Jennifer Killick has written three books for children, *Alex Sparrow and the Really Big Stink* (Firefly 2017) *Alex Sparrow and the Furry Fury* (2018) and *Mo, Lottie and the Junkers* (2019) all of which have been selected for the Summer Reading Challenge. She had always wanted to be a writer, but really started when she took a Creative Writing MA at Brunel University, which is where she first got the idea for 'Alex Sparrow'. Jennifer lives in Uxbridge, in a house full of children, animals and Lego. When she isn't busy mothering or stepmothering (which isn't often) she loves to read, write and run, as fast as she can.

ALEX SPARROW
and the Zumbie Apocalypse

by Jennifer Killick

First published in 2019
by Firefly Press
25 Gabalfa Road, Llandaff North, Cardiff, CF14 2JJ
www.fireflypress.co.uk

A CIP catalogue record of this book is available from the British Library.

ISBN 978-1-913102-04-3

This book has been published with the support of the Welsh Books Council.

Typeset by: Elaine Sharples
Original cover art by Heath McKenzie

Printed and bound in Great Britain by Clays Ltd, Elcograph S.p.A

For Mum, Dad, Julie and David – thank you
for a lifetime of Christmas memories.

1

The Very Surprising Funeral

'Alex, switch it off!' Jess hissed at me as another searing fart bubbled in my ear. 'We've only been here ten minutes and people are already desperate to get away from us. Look how far they've all shuffled.'

I inspected the widening gap between us and the other people on our bench. 'It's no bad thing, Jessticles. They're all squashed together and we have stretching room – look.'

I swung my arms around as if I was doing an

agent warm-up exercise (as recommended before undertaking any mission in the Awesome Agent Alex Academy handbook), accidentally bumping the shoulder of the lady in front of me and making her drop her sucky sweets, which scattered all over the floor. Jess huffed and folded her arms.

I'd never been to a funeral before and hadn't especially wanted to, but Mum said I was old enough to 'pay my respects', whatever the heck that means, to Mrs Spires from next-door-but-one because she gave me twenty pence once when I pulled all the stinging nettles out of her garden for her. It was the worst job ever. It was super-hot and I got stung a gazillion times, so probably worth at least two pounds. But I got twenty pence and a glass of warm tap water.

Anyway, she died last week, something to do with her heart, Mum said. It was sad, and Mum and Nanny Sparrow were upset because they went to Zumba class with her and it happened right in front of them. So I saw why they would want to go to the funeral, but I didn't see why I had to. It was mostly full of old people, lots of them crying, and it made me uncomfortable. I'd suffered enough with the stinging nettles.

'She was a kind-hearted lady who would do anything for anyone.' A man in a suit was standing at the front, reading from a bit of paper. My ear farted again, as it does every time someone tells a lie. Thanks to The Professor (aka Miss Fortress), who gave me my rather smelly superpower, I'm a sort of human lie-detector! I held in a snigger as the stink poured out.

'Alex!' Jess glared at me.

We were in a big room with rows of benches and a pathway down the middle, leading from the door to the front, like someone was about to get married. At the front was a platform with a table on it, covered in candles and flowers. Actually, that was kind of like a wedding, too. Why do they do weddings and funerals the same? That makes no sense at all. I'm pretty certain I'll never have a wedding, but if I ever have a funeral, I want it to be dark, with everyone holding a lightsaber in an imperial salute, and my coffin being carried up the pathway to Darth Vader's music.

'Why are you humming?' Jess hissed.

'I'm not humming, I'm sound-tracking. When our story is made into a movie, and it *will* be made into a movie, we need to make sure we have all the important things covered.' In the last three months, me and Jess had both got weird superpowers, learned how to use them, stopped an evil teacher at our school, taken down a lab that was doing illegal tests on animals, and avoided being destroyed by our nemesis, Montgomery McMonaghan. If anyone deserved a movie being made about them, it was me. And Jess, I suppose.

'And what are the important things?'

'I'm glad you asked that, Jessticles. I have a list.'

'Of course you do,' Jess sighed.

'If a movie is going to be properly awesome, it needs the following things: number one, zombies.'

'So that's out straight away,' Jess said. 'What else?'

'Number two, sick soundtrack. Number three, cool gadgets. Number four, epic chase scene.'

'Right.' Jess rolled her eyes.

'Number five, plot twist. Number six, heart-warming moment. Number seven, a shark and-slash-or an octopus. And number eight, the ultimate death through sacrifice.'

'We literally have none of those things.'

'We have none of those things *yet*,' I said. 'Patience, Jessticles.'

'Cos we're going to somehow come across a zombie and an octopus,' Jess said.

'Shush.' The old lady in front of us turned around and glared.

'Yeah, shush, Jess – this is a funeral,' I said.

Mrs Spires' coffin was white, and there was a dome of red and white flowers on top.

'Why is there a photo of a random woman next to Mrs Spires' coffin?' I whispered.

'That's Mrs Spires, idiot.'

'It never is.'

'Of course it is. Who else would it be? Beyoncé?'

I leaned forward to get a better look, but we were too far away. Mum and Nanny Sparrow were sitting towards the front of the room, but I convinced them that me and Jess should sit at the back, in case it got too much for us. Really it was just so we could chat and because I didn't want to sit with Mum and Nanny. They're so embarrassing. Mum was going to say no, but Nanny butted in and said, 'Good idea, Alex. Sometimes one needs a breath of air at a time like this.'

I nodded wisely, in the manner of someone

much maturer than their age, even though I thought it was stupid.

'Why do people say to get a "breath of air"?' I whispered to Jess. 'What else are you going to breathe? Ketchup?'

'Right now, all I'm breathing is your stink,' she said. 'Switch your lie-detector off or the rest of the funeral is going to be unbearable.'

'It's not my fault everyone's pretending Mrs Spires was nice when she wasn't.'

'But it's disrespectful to be making that awful smell at her funeral. She wasn't *that* bad.'

My ear farted again and I sniggered.

'Liar, liar, pants on fire,' I said.

Jess's cheeks turned pink. She never usually lies about anything.

'All those times you walked Snuffles for her,' I said. (Snuffles was Mrs Spires' dog.) 'In the rain, in the snow, when you had loads of homework, when you had a cold. And how did she show her gratitude?'

'She cooked me dinner once when my mum was stuck at work,' Jess said.

'And what did she cook you?'

Jess wriggled in her seat. Unfolded and re-folded her arms. Bit her lip, sighed and said, 'Liver.'

'She knew you were a vegan, did she not?'

'Yes,' Jess said.

'And what were her thoughts on that, hmmm?'

'She said to stop being so silly and eat what she'd made me, or she'd tell my mum that I was an ungrateful child.'

'How did that make you feel?'

Jess made a face. 'OK, fine, so I didn't like her,' she said, her voice a little louder but drowned out to everyone except me by the song they were all singing really, *really* badly. 'But just because she was horrid doesn't mean I'm glad she's dead.'

Unfortunately for Jess, the song ended at the exact moment she said the last part of that sentence – the 'I'm glad she's dead' part.

A bunch of heads turned round to give her the most disgusted looks I've ever seen. And I've seen a lot of disgusted looks. People tutted and shook their heads, the feathers and weird fishing-net stuff wobbling on their hats. Jess slid down in her seat, her face red like the fiery sun.

There was only one thing I could do. I stuffed my hat in my mouth and bit on it hard to stop myself from laughing.

'Shut up,' she said.

'Let us take a moment to reflect in silence on what Rose meant to us,' the head funeral guy said, and everyone looked at the floor. The room was deathly quiet. Ooh – deathly quiet – get it? I was just about to lean over to whisper my pun to Jess. I was working very hard on puns because all good agents, especially the ones in movies, can wordplay as well as extract important information from criminals and cage fight with gorillas. But I was distracted by a knocking sound.

At first I thought I had imagined it. It was muffled and distant and nobody else seemed to have noticed. But then it came again – tap, tap, tap. People started to look up from their silent reflection and glance around. The knocking became louder and it was definitely coming from the front of the room.

'What is that?' Jess said.

'I think someone's trying to beatbox,' I said.

'Maybe someone forgot to put their phone on silent,' said Jess, completely ignoring my suggestion, as if it was ridiculous.

'Lame ringtone,' I snorted. Mine was 'Duel of the Fates' from *Star Wars*. Every time my phone went off, I got to pretend I was Darth Maul fighting Obi-Wan and Qui-Gon Jinn with my bad-A double-ended lightsaber.

'Turn it off!' someone shouted. 'Whose is it?'

'It's coming from the front!' someone else called, and people started looking towards where Mum and Nanny Sparrow were sitting. Mum was rummaging in her bag in case it was hers, even though she knew it wasn't because she has the boring ring-ring ringtone.

The funeral boss put his hands up. 'Could the owner of the phone please silence it?' he said. 'This is a funeral.'

Then the knocking was joined by a wailing noise. It sounded like someone was shouting from far away.

'What the devil is that?' a man in front of us said, and then everyone started talking crossly.

'For goodness' sake, shush.' Nanny Sparrow stood up and glared round at everyone. 'Let's just listen so we can get to the bottom of this, shall we?'

Everyone fell silent – Nanny Sparrow is not someone to be messed with.

There was a moment of nothing, and then the knocking began again, louder and quicker, and definitely with a voice. We all strained to hear.

'Must be a ghost,' I said. 'Or a zombie.'

'Don't be stupid, Alex.'

'What's it saying?' said the man who had read out the speech of lies about Mrs Spires.

The funeral boss guy took a step nearer to the coffin and looked at it in horror. We all watched as he took another step towards it. 'I … I think it's coming from here,' he said.

'Absurd!' someone shouted. 'What is this nonsense? Call this a funeral?'

Funeral boss looked scared.

'Put your ear to the coffin,' I shouted in my best attempt at an old lady voice, which I thought was very authentic.

Jess nudged me hard in the ribs.

'Yes, put your ear to it, man. We need to know what's going on here,' Nanny joined in. Everyone else was shouting in agreement.

Funeral boss was shaking as he edged towards the coffin, like it was going to come to life and eat him. He leant over and put his ear to it. Silence. And then a distant, but definite, wailing noise.

The guy jumped back in absolute horror. 'It's coming from inside the coffin,' he said, his eyes wide and sweat gleaming on his forehead.

'It can't be, Paul,' another man charged over from the corner. 'Let me have a go.'

Paul stood to one side, pulling at his tie, and the second guy put his ear to the coffin. There was a knock so loud and hard that the weird dome of flowers actually moved. The second guy whispered something to Paul.

'What on earth is going on?' Nanny Sparrow shouted.

Paul turned to the audience. 'Please accept my apologies, but we're going to have a short intermission while we complete some, err, last-minute checks.'

Everyone stood up and started to shout. I wished I was nearer the front so I could get a better look. It was all Mum and Nanny Sparrow's fault that I was stuck back here away from the action – any responsible adult would have forced me to sit with them, in case I got upset.

Paul pressed some hidden button and two thick blue curtains, like they have at the cinema, moved along a rail towards each other to block off the platform.

'Unfair,' I said. 'I think they're going to open the coffin.'

'Grow up, Alex. Do you really want to see a dead body?' Jess stood up next to me, trying a bit too hard not to look towards the curtains.

'It's not a dead body, Jessticles. Dead bodies can't knock on lids, or make weird noises with their mouths. Unless...'

'Don't even say it, Alex. Just, don't.'

'Zombie,' I said. 'Mrs Spires is a zombie.'

'That's impossible,' Jess huffed.

'Yeah, but we've seen quite a lot of the impossible lately, haven't we?' I said. 'Loads of things that couldn't happen in real life, but that *are* happening in real life. Our superpowers. Blueberried children. Warlord cats. Guinea pigs who can text.' Since our teacher Miss Fortress had given us our powers, we'd faced a bunch of the weirdest, most dangerous situations ever.

'Everyone please leave the chapel by the closest exit,' Paul was shouting above the excited chatter. 'As a matter of urgency.'

A couple of other funeral people started directing everyone towards the doors and, though I didn't want to leave, Jess and me were sucked up by the herd. I could hear the drone of an electric drill whirring behind the curtain.

'They're opening it!' I said.

'Oh flip, they actually are.' Jess looked back over her shoulder, but all we could see were the velvet curtains of blindness and concealment.

Everyone was crushing together. There were strange smells around me that I couldn't label, other than to say there were odours of flowers, soup and cardigans in there.

'Ugh, I wish people would stop squashing together,' Jess said, as she got whacked in the face with a handbag.

'Me too, I need a breath of air,' I said. 'Hang on … Mrs Spires was a friendly and generous person.' I said that last bit loudly.

People turned to smile at me, but their expressions quickly changed as they smelt the stink my lie had created. They scowled at Jess and pushed away from us.

'Oh no, they think it was me!' Jess said.

'It's because you're so disrespectful at funerals,' I sighed. 'Now let's get outside and talk zombies.'

We finally made it out into the freezing air.

'She's not a zombie, Double-O-Delusional.' Jess pulled her coat on and did up the zip.

'Just because you hated her so much you

shouted something rude at her funeral, does not mean that she isn't a zombie. I need to think up a new sidekick name for you.'

'Well, we'll soon find out. If she really is a zombie, she'll bite Paul and the other people that work here, and they'll all come out and attack us.'

'Son of a biscuit, you're right for once!' I said, stuffing my hand into my pocket and feeling around. 'Luckily for you, I brought a gadget-slash-weapon, which also means we have item three from the list ticked off.'

'Why would you bring a weapon to a funeral?' Jess said.

'I ordered it from the internet a week ago. I was just about to test it this morning when Mum walked in. I knew she wouldn't want me having something so dangerous, so I hid it in my pocket. And a good thing I did.'

'Where even are your mum and nan? They're going to be looking for us – we should find them.'

'No, Jessticles. Mum and Nanny are old and weak. If the zombies are coming – and they *are* coming – they'll only slow us down.'

'Nice.' Jess looked at me like I'd just punched a kitten.

I was about to show Jess my new and incredibly cool weapon, when Mum and Nanny Sparrow pushed through the crowd towards us.

'Come on, Alex, we're getting in the car.'

'But I don't want to go home yet, I need to know what's going on.' I side-eyed Jess. 'It could be a matter of national security.'

'We're not going home, love. We're going to the wake.' Nanny put her arm around me.

'You see, Jess, this happens so often that they even have a name for it.'

'What happens so often, Alex?' Nanny said.

'You know, when dead bodies wake up.'

Mum and Nanny laughed. 'A wake is what you call the gathering after a funeral ceremony,' Mum said. 'Where we all get together and remember the person we've lost.'

'You thought we were going to watch Mrs Spires climbing out of her coffin, didn't you?' Jess sniggered.

'No,' I said, my stink cutting through the frosty air. 'Because it makes so much sense to have a party after someone has died. I'm staying here until I know what's going on.' I put my agent foot down. 'Where do you even have these alleged funeral parties, anyway?'

'At the cricket club,' Mum said. 'There will be a buffet.'

'What are we waiting for? Off to the car!' And I ran ahead as fast as I could across the icy ground.

2

The Cricket Club of Destiny and The One with No Name

I managed to get to the buffet, pile my plate high with food, and get a drink before everything got contaminated with people's unwashed toilet hands. I dibsed us a table in the corner and sat down with my lunch, most of which involved meat in pastry and cubes of things on sticks. Jess had a pathetic-looking plate of carrot coins and celery shards. I looked around at the cricket club. Since the shiny new leisure centre had opened down the road, it didn't get used for sports much, except for cricket in the summer. But whenever anyone had any kind of party in Cherry Tree Lane, they pretty much always had it here. It was really big, with loads of tables and chairs and a massive snooker table in one corner. It was also the least fancy place in town. Everything in it was brown-coloured, even the manky cat that always hung out there. It was decorated for Christmas now, with multi-coloured lights and tinsel draped across the walls, but somehow it still gave me an overwhelming sense of brown.

'How's Meena doing now?' I asked between mouthfuls. Meena was a German Shepherd dog that had belonged to an animal scientist called Taran (who Jess had a massive crush on when she met him, as I like to remind her). He pretended he was awesome, and he wore cool cardigans, but it turned out he was stealing animals and doing awful things to them in his experiments for McMonaghan. After we defeated him at the animal-testing SPARC laboratory, Meena was taken into care. But she'd been so brave, protecting us from Taran and helping us escape, we couldn't leave her in a foster home. So Jess had adopted her.

Jess swallowed a chunk of raw carrot. 'She's still clingy. She's happy as long as I'm there but she gets scared whenever I go out without her. How about Mr Prickles?'

'His spines are growing back nicely and his sore bits are all better, but he has nightmares when he sleeps. He makes these squeaking noises that sound like crying. It's awful.' My hedgehog, the awesome Mr Prickles, was one of the smallest, and bravest, victims of Taran and his shady boss at SPARC, the evil genius Montgomery McMonaghan.

'Montgomery McMonaghan is responsible for so much suffering,' said Jess.

'Yeah, it seems like every time something bad goes down in Cherry Tree Lane, he's behind it. He turned half the school into blueberries – I mean brainwashed the pupils, with his sidekick teacher Miss Smilie – then started on the local animals with SPARC. What is his beef with our town?'

Jess started to twitch. She only twitched when she was using her own superpower – communicating with animals.

'Honestly, Jessticles, I know you think I eat like a pig, but there's no need to talk to me like one. Rude.'

'I'm not talking to you,' Jess said. 'I'm talking to her.' She pointed at the manky cricket club cat. 'She wants us to follow her.'

I looked at the cat, who was chocolate brown and crazy fluffy. There was also a crazy look in her eyes which made me definitely *not* want to follow her anywhere.

'You go,' I said. 'There's a trifle the size of a bath over there, and I intend to eat at least half of it.'

'She said she has information about "that which we seek".'

I sighed, and prayed to Thor, god of thunder and over-eating, that the trifle would be intact when we returned, and then we followed the cat out of the main room and down some narrow stairs. As the door closed behind us, the sound of the party – clinking glasses and old people chatter – faded to almost nothing. The lights in the stairwell sputtered, and an icy breeze followed us, even though there weren't any open windows. The cat had, apparently, agreed to spare us a few moments of her time, but only if we helped her prepare.

'Prepare for what, though, Jess?' I whispered. 'A less courageous and experienced agent might find this a bit creepy.'

'We can't have a proper talk with her in front of everyone,' Jess hissed back. 'She said she can help us. What choice do we have?'

Since our dealings with Boris and Noodle, the school guinea pigs of treachery, we'd become more suspicious of animals we didn't know. Like people, they were complicated. Like people, they could have hidden agendas.

This cat might once have been fancy, but her fur was tangled and she had a slight limp. We followed her down winding corridors, all cold and empty, the smell of old sweat lingering in the air. I was still half expecting the start of the zombie outbreak, so I kept my hand on the weapon in my pocket. Jess didn't look scared at all, and that made me feel better.

The cat pushed through some double doors and we found ourselves in a changing room. The women's changing room.

'Maybe I should wait outside,' I said, assessing the room for escape routes and not finding any.

'Don't be stupid. I don't think anyone's used this as a changing room for months.'

I turned to the cat. 'Thanks for bringing us to this totally non-creepy basement changing room with no fire exits. What's your name?'

Jess twitched away as the cat sat in front of a full-length mirror and started preening herself.

'Tell me what she's saying, Jess. I am the top agent, so I should hear everything.'

'Why don't you shut up so I can listen?'

'Unfair.' I poked her in the arm.

'Stop it!' Jess whacked me.

'Tell me, then,' I said. 'Every word.'

'I'll tell you every word … ish.'

'That'll do, my raging friend.'

'OK, here we go…'

'Wait,' I said. 'What's her voice like?'

'Think wistful, kind of husky, like she has a bit of a sore throat.' Jess turned to the cat. 'Does that sound right?' She juddered away for a few seconds, then turned back to me. 'She told me to say that her voice is full of the tears of bittersweet memories and a roughness that reflects the hardships she has endured.'

Blimey. 'Got it,' I said.

'She doesn't have a name. She had one once, but that was a lifetime ago, during happier days when she was loved.'

'Oh.' I didn't say it out loud because I've learnt a lot about offending animals, but I was starting to regret demanding the full-length version from Jess.

'She used to be audacious. Special. She wouldn't get out of bed for anything less than the finest smoked salmon. Now she must live amongst the dregs of society, begging for scraps, performing like a common entertainer.'

'That's too bad,' I said, wanting to hurry things along a bit.

Jess juddered away again. 'She was beloved by her human companion and they resided with a mutual respect and affection, until a cruel twist of fate separated them. Her name was lost with her companion and her pride.'

'And that was how long ago?'

'Two years to a human,' Jess said. 'A lifetime to a cat.'

'That's weird – I'm sure there's been a cat here for longer than that.'

The cat made a wheezing noise and shook her head.

'She's laughing,' Jess said. 'She says there has always been and will always be a cat here. This is a hub, a meeting place for lost souls. Some pass through, others stay until they find what they're looking for. When she moves on – and she will move on when her human companion returns for her – another will take her place.'

Jeez. This was more depressing than the funeral.

'Um, I hope your human companion finds you soon,' I said. 'But why have you brought us here?'

'Hold on,' Jess said. 'She wants me to floof her tail.'

'What?'

'Floof her tail.' Jess started combing the cat with no name's tail with her fingers, gently pulling the hair the wrong way so the tail looked extra fluffy.

'Err, why?'

'Because she's preparing for her performance. She overheard us talking and has something to show us. All we need to do, is – erm – wait for her performance, and follow.'

The cat stood and prowled out of the room.

'Not gonna lie, Jess, this is the weirdest situation ever. And we've been in some weird situations.'

'Yeah.' Jess shrugged. 'We'd better follow her.'

We followed the cat back through the corridors towards the funeral party again. We opened the door to find that the buffet had been demolished, and everyone was a lot louder than they had been. There were empty wine glasses everywhere, and a queue at the bar.

'The cat says we should wait at the jukebox and be ready to load up song number E95,' Jess said.

We crossed to the corner of the room where the jukebox stood flashing wildly, like it was desperate to be unleashed. Someone had put a Santa hat on top of its domed head. I examined the song list.

'Are you sure about this?' I said. 'That song doesn't really seem appropriate for a funeral.'

Jess jerked around, then shrugged again. 'She says she's been in this business long enough to read a room. When the time comes, load the song and follow.'

Just then, a man I'd seen at the funeral burst in through the door.

'Can I have your attention, everyone?' he shouted. He was sweating, his tie lopsided and a huge grin on his face. 'I have news – miraculous news! She's not dead. Rose isn't dead!'

There was a gasp from the room and a moment of silence while everyone stared at the man.

'There was a freak, one-in-a-million mistake,' the man said. 'She was just in some sort of heavily unconscious state. She's been taken to hospital to be checked over, but she seems completely fine. She's not dead.'

Everyone started chattering at the same time, not knowing whether to be shocked, happy or angry.

'Thanks so much to you all for being here,' the man said. 'On behalf of Rose and the family, I'd like you all to enjoy the buffet and a drink on us.'

Everyone cheered.

'Now someone get me a pint,' the man laughed. 'Let's celebrate!'

The cat nodded at me, so I punched the code into the jukebox.

Some tropical party music began to play. The cat bounced forward and Jess started to twitch. 'Grab my waist, we've got to get the conga line going and then she'll lead us to the truth.'

'Seriously?'

But Jess was already jolting forward, half twitching in conversation with the cat and, I think, half dancing, though it was hard to tell. I put my hands on her waist, which I really didn't want to do, and shouted, 'Come on everyone, let's conga for Mrs Spires!' Unbelievably, people started to join the line, whooping and singing. We weaved our way around the room, following the cat, until Jess broke away and said, 'This is where we get off.'

We stopped in front of a wall of photographs, panting and sweating, as the line of drunken adults carried on past the bar, with some of them laughing at our 'lack of stamina'.

'So, what are we looking at?' I said.

'This.' Jess pointed at a photo. It was of a group of men and boys and girls dressed in cricket clothes, smiling and posing with their bats. Underneath it said "Sinha, Wilkinson, McMonaghan, Patel, Kennedy and Cetinay, celebrating their victory."

'McMonaghan,' I said, peering at the photo. 'It couldn't be, could it?'.

'Look, there!' Jess tapped the glass. 'It looks just like him. Montgomery McMonaghan. He plays cricket in Cherry Tree Lane, or at least he used to. He's connected to the town.'

'Finally, a clue!' I said.

'Alex, we weren't even looking for clues. Don't you think this is weirdly convenient?'

'No. It's because I am an awesome agent. Now

how are we going to steal this photo? The frame's quite big and looks heavy, but I could probably smuggle it out under my coat.'

'Or we could do this,' Jess said, holding up her phone and taking a photograph of the photograph. She looked at me in disgust.

We walked back over to our table and sat down.

'Weirdest day ever,' Jess said, taking a sip of her lemonade.

3

Return of The Spires

A few days after the funeral that turned out not to be a funeral, me and Jess sat at the breakfast bar in my kitchen, looking at the photo on her phone.

'It kind of looks like an old photo,' I said, 'but Montgomery McMonaghan looks about the same age as he does now.'

'Yeah, I thought that too.'

'You know what this means?' I looked at Jess.

'I'm sure you're going to tell me what you think it means, and I'm sure it's going to be idiotic.'

'All his experimenting,' I said. 'The brainwashing of kids and the testing on animals. He's found the secret to immortality. He's actually three hundred years old.'

Jess rolled her eyes. 'Like I said. Idiotic.'

'It's classic super-villain stuff, though. They all want to live for ever; it's part of the job description.'

'What do you think, Bob?' Jess said, showing him the picture as he swam a circuit of the fish tank he shared with Elle. Bob, although a goldfish, had been a vital agent in our adventures, and was excellent at noticing things that our pathetic human eyes couldn't.

'It's sick to have a clue about McMonaghan's links to Cherry Tree Lane, but I don't really know what we can do with it,' I sighed.

'Alex!' Mum's voice made me jump as she walked into the kitchen. Jess dropped her phone.

'Mrs Spires came home from the hospital this morning, and her children have had to go back to Cornwall. Can you and Jess just pop in on her and make sure she's OK?'

'We're a bit busy, actually, Mum,' I said. 'Can't you go?'

'I have to take Lauren to ballet, and your dad is working late. Be a good boy and just spend half an hour with her, she's been through a lot.'

'How about Lauren just skips ballet? She dances like a flipping elephant, anyway,' I said, annoyed that Mum was making me do something useful and still a bit worried that Mrs Spires would try to eat my brain.

'Of course we'll go, Mrs Sparrow,' Jess said, giving me the stink-eye. 'Come on, Alex.'

I scraped my stool back as angrily as I could. Mum pretended she didn't notice and kissed me on top of my head.

'Just grabbing something from my room,' I said, darting past her and up the stairs. Making sure nobody was watching except Mr Prickles, who I could trust with the most secretey secrets in the world, I took my new weapon from its hiding place and put it in my pocket, being careful not to activate it. Mr P had been snoozing in his nest, but he looked up at me with his cute little face as I banged around.

'I really want to take you, Mr Prickles,' I said, tickling him under his chin, 'but I have to make sure Mrs Spires isn't dangerous first. Your prickles aren't strong enough to protect you yet and I'd never forgive myself if she ate you.'

He nodded and licked my hand, and I knew he understood. The truth was that I'd been scared to take him out anywhere since he'd been half-killed by Taran. I gave him a handful of hedgehog treats and ran back downstairs.

Me and Jess strudged down the road towards Mrs Spires' house. Strudging is the kind of walk you do when you don't want to go somewhere, and you're making it take as long as possible, like a slow trudge. Neither of us really wanted to spend time alone with a mean old lady who was probably going to rip our insides out and suck on them for dinner. It was already getting dark, and people's Christmas lights were flickering on. I usually loved this time of year, but things just felt off.

'As we walk to our destiny, and probably our doom, I want you to know, dear Jessticles, that there's no one I'd rather have by my side.'

'Why does everything you say sound like a cheesy Hollywood tagline, lately?' Jess sighed.

'They'll want all our best lines for the movie.'

'They'll cut that one, then,' Jess snorted. She

rang Mrs Spires' doorbell. We heard some shouting and barking coming from behind the front door. As the door opened, we saw Snuffles' scraggly bottom scampering up the stairs.

'Oh, it's you two,' Mrs Spires said, in a very anti-climaxy way. 'You'd better come in.'

We followed her down the hall and into her lounge. I used my super-agent eyes to assess Mrs Spires from behind.

'Is she walking funny?' I whispered to Jess. 'Dragging her leg a bit?'

'She's not a zombie,' Jess whispered back.

'Sit down.' Mrs Spires pointed to the sofa. 'I'll get you a glass of milk. It's been in my fridge for days and starting to turn. Don't want to waste it.'

'Err, thanks?' I said.

'Why is Snuffles upstairs?' Jess looked around the room. 'He's usually in here in his special chair.'

'Stupid dog won't come near me since I got back from hospital.' Mrs Spires tutted as she left the room.

I nudged Jess. 'He knows.'

Mrs Spires put our glasses on coasters on the table and stood by the TV, which was turned on with the volume right up.

'Don't you need to sit down, Mrs Spires?' Jess said.

'I'm not dead, you know. I've never felt better.'

She sort of rubbed against the TV in a way that made me uncomfortable.

'I'll be back at Zumba tomorrow,' she said. 'I need to catch up on all the gossip I've missed.' She walked to the corner and bent over to switch on a lamp. 'I heard Mamie had a turn. They thought they'd lost her – out for ten minutes 'til they brought her back in the ambulance,' Mrs Spires said, turning on another lamp. 'Of course, she's only in the beginners' class, so she probably overdid it.'

'Two people collapsing in Zumba,' I said. 'That's a strange coincidence.'

'Three people,' Mrs Spires said. 'Pat from the Tuesday class went down too.'

'Is she OK?' Jess said.

'Right as rain. Only technically dead for a second. Drink your milk up.'

I put my glass to my mouth and pretended to take a sip. No way was I swallowing gone-off milk.

'I heard Mamie had a turn,' said Mrs Spires, turning on the radio. 'They thought they'd lost her.'

Me and Jess looked at each other. Mrs Spires wandered out of the room, muttering, 'Beginners' class. Probably overdid it.'

'Mrs Spires, I'm just going to check on Snuffles,' Jess called out.

I nudged Jess hard in the ribs. 'Don't leave me,' I mouthed.

Jess shrugged. 'Keep her distracted,' she whispered, and walked off.

I tipped my mouldy milk into a plant pot but left Jess's on the table. I zipped up my coat as Mrs Spires came back into the room with a toaster.

'Aren't you cold?' I said. 'It's usually really hot in your house but it's freezing right now. Aren't your radiators working?'

'Gas boiler,' she said. 'Working fine, just don't need it on. I don't feel cold. You probably need to drink more milk.'

'I'm good, thanks,' I said, watching with a really horrible feeling as she plugged in the toaster. I put my hand in my pocket and squeezed my weapon.

With the radio and TV on loud, I didn't notice Jess coming back until she was in the room. She gave me a look.

'We should probably get going, Mrs Spires,' I said. 'If you're sure you're OK.'

'Do you want a doctor's note or something? I'm in perfect health,' she snapped, walking out of the room and returning with a kettle.

My ear said she was telling the truth, but my eyes were telling me that something was seriously up.

'Kettle?' Jess mouthed at me behind Mrs Spires' back.

I rolled my eyes across to the toaster, which was on the carpet next to the lit-up Christmas tree. Jess's eyes got super-wide.

'Not enough poxy sockets,' Mrs Spires said, dangling the wire of the kettle from her hand. 'I'd better get down the shops and buy an extension lead. You two will have to go.'

'Um, OK,' I said, jumping off the sofa.

'Did you want some milk before you leave? It's been in my fridge for days and starting to turn. Don't want to waste it.'

'I've finished mine,' I said. 'Jess hasn't, though. She's so wasteful.'

'Kids these days have no idea of the value of things,' Mrs Spires tutted, picking a lamp off the sideboard and stroking her face with it.

'Bye, Mrs Spires,' Jess said. I was one step ahead of her, practically running down the hall.

As soon as the door was shut behind us, I turned to Jess. 'She's eaten him, hasn't she?'

'Eaten who?'

'Snuffles. I saw your face when you came downstairs.'

'No, she hasn't eaten him, dummy.'

'Then what was the face for? I know your resting, moody face, and this was different.'

'Snuffles was scared. He kept saying that she's not the same. She smells funny. That she's come back different.'

'Do you know what this means?'

'Alex, she isn't a zombie – she didn't try to eat us.'

'You're disappointed, I can tell,' I said.

'Why would I be disappointed that Mrs Spires didn't try to eat us?' Jess's voice went really high.

'Let's not give up hope yet, Jessticles.'

'So we're hoping that she tries to eat us?

'Of course, because, one – she was dead and now she's not, and two – her beloved pet dog no longer recognises her as the owner he used to adore. These are both classic symptoms of zombieism.'

'But...'

'And it would be so boring if Mrs Spires was just a normal zombie – the kind you see every day...'

'We've literally never seen a...'

'So we get the added bonus of some intriguing new crazy behaviours: one – repeating half of what she said, in exactly the same way, over and over again without realising.'

'She did seem to be stuck in some kind of loop,' Jess sighed.

'And two...' I held up two gloved fingers '...the plugging in everything electrical and rubbing herself against it like a cat. That was my favourite part.'

'Favourite?' Jess snorted. 'You were terrified.'

'A good agent allows himself just the right amount of fear to ensure that he is always alert. What you saw was me being an awesome agent, not me freaking out.'

That created an especially manurery fart.

'Why, though? Why would she stroke her face with a lamp?' Jess said, as I rang my front doorbell.

'That, my twitching teammate, is what we need

to find out. Do you know what this is?' I wiggled my eyebrows at her.

'Yeah, yeah, a mission, blah, blah, blah.'

'Though it is ever so cold outside, Jessticles, you talking that way has filled my heart with warmth.'

'That one's definitely not making it into the movie.' She rolled her eyes.

'Too cringe?'

'Like, a million times over.'

'But it's Christmas!'

My mum opened the door with a hundred questions about Mrs Spires, and our mission talk was over for the day.

4

Bothering Miss Fortress

'Can't this wait? I only have ten minutes left of break and I need more coffee.'

Me and Jess looked at each other.

Miss Fortress had been in a really stinky mood lately, but today seemed especially bad. I decided not to mention the fact that she already had a full cup of coffee in her hand.

'We wouldn't bother you if it wasn't life or death stuff, Miss,' I said, trying to do cute puppy eyes like my little sister does to my mum.

'Did you contract a rare, life-threatening disease that causes the sufferer to develop crazed facial expressions?'

'Err no.' (Note for the Agent Alex handbook – need to practise my adorable face in the mirror before I wheel it out in public again.) 'But it is a sort of medical thing.'

'You should make an appointment with your GP. I'm not that type of doctor.'

'Would you just get over yourself for a minute and listen?' Jess shouted suddenly, thumping her hand down on the desk. 'This is important and we need your help.'

Miss Fortress looked up, clearly trying to decide whether to tell Jess off, or actually listen to what we had to say. It was a tense moment. Finally, she put her cup down and sighed. 'Go on.'

I tried to think of a way to sum it up so we could get the conversation done quickly and not pee her off any more than we already had. 'So, basically, there's a zombie invasion starting and we need to know what to do.'

'Jess,' Miss Fortress said, not looking the slightest bit alarmed. 'Maybe you should tell me.'

I huffed and plonked myself down in a chair. No doubt Jess would find the boringest way ever to tell it.

'Alex and I went to the funeral of an old lady we knew. She collapsed in Zumba and they thought she'd had a heart attack. During the funeral there was a knocking from inside her coffin and it turns out she was alive.'

'That is unusual,' Miss Fortress said, 'but not unheard of. Probably some poor doctor made a mistake after a forty-hour shift.'

'But she's not the only one,' Jess said. 'Two other ladies…'

'That we know of, Jessticles, that we know of,' I said.

'…have also suddenly collapsed in Zumba classes and been technically dead for at least a few seconds before coming back.'

'Could be a coincidence,' Miss Fortress said. 'I've never been to a Zumba class, but I understand they're physically demanding.'

'How can they be demanding?' I said. 'My mum and nanny do it. It's just a bit of swaying about, they hardly even move off the spot.'

'For someone who's been proven wrong many

times, your blind confidence that you're always right is almost impressive,' Miss Fortress said.

'I know, right?' I smiled.

Jess did a hard eye-roll. 'But there's a bit more to it. We spent some time with Mrs Spires, the lady...'

'Zombie,' I whispered.

'...the *lady* who came back to life at her funeral, and there were a few things that didn't seem right.'

'Did she suddenly start finding Alex's jokes hilarious?' Miss Fortress said.

'Ooh, sick burn,' I held my fist up. 'Knuckles for that, Miss F.'

Miss Fortress ignored me.

'She kept repeating herself, but not in the usual forgetful way that people do sometimes. It was more like...'

'She was stuck in a memory loop,' I said. 'And that wasn't even the weirdest thing.'

'Her dog wouldn't go anywhere near her. When I spoke to him he seemed really scared – he said she smelt strange and that she was different somehow.'

'And then there's the absolute best weird part,' I said.

'She had everything electrical in the house switched on. She brought most of her appliances into the lounge, and she was...'

'Rubbing herself on them,' I said.

'She was what?' Miss Fortress finally looked surprised.

'Like a cat against someone with a pocket full of fish,' I said.

'Gross,' Jess said. 'But true.'

'That does sound odd.' Miss Fortress frowned. 'I can't think what could have caused it. I'll look into it but, in the meantime, I suggest you investigate.'

'Yesssss!' I jumped out of my chair, bumping the desk and knocking over Miss Fortress's coffee. 'Oh fudge,' I said.

'For goodness' sake,' Miss Fortress said, and she didn't even shout like usual. She said it all quietly and sadly, and looked like she was going to cry.

'Sorry, Miss,' I said.

'Wait there,' she sniffed, wiping at the spilt coffee with the class art-project pictures. 'I'm getting more coffee; I'll be back in a minute.'

She left the room without throwing anything at us.

'She doesn't seem right at the moment,' I said to Jess as we sat in the empty classroom.

'Yeah, it's like she's lost her spark.'

'Do you think the fact that she replaced her chewed-up Science Is Sexy travel cup with a unicorn one is a bad sign?'

'Of course it's a bad sign. She HATES mythical creatures. She must have just picked up the first one she saw in the shop.'

'The other day I walked in unexpectedly, and I swear she was talking to a picture.'

'What picture?'

'The one she has as her screensaver, of the guy who plays Superman wearing a really tight jumper.' I pulled a bag of Percy Pigs out of my pocket and put two in my mouth.

'Did you know Percy Pigs are vegan?' Jess said.

'Oh, are they? You can have some if you like.' I'd chosen them deliberately because they're vegan and I could share them with Jess. I didn't want her to know that, though. I had my hard-man reputation to think about.

'Well, it's obvious what's wrong with her, isn't it?' Jess said, chewing on a sweet.

‘I thought so, but I didn’t want to say.’

‘We’ll have to try to think of something we can do about it,’ Jess sighed.

‘Don’t worry, I have a plan. We just need some strong rope, a bottle of holy water and an online course about how to become a priest.’

Jess looked at me in what seemed suspiciously like disgust. ‘What the hell are you talking about?’

‘For the exorcism, obvs.’

‘Err, why?’

I was starting to think that me and Jess weren’t thinking the same thing at all. ‘Because she’s possessed by an evil spirit. That’s what’s wrong with her, right?’

‘Oh god, Alex, just when I think you can’t get any more deluded!’

‘Do you have a better theory?’ I said.

‘Err, yes. She’s stressed about Montgomery McMonaghan maybe finding out where she is.’

I nodded. They had serious beef because she ditched him when he turned evil, and he was a dangerous son of a biscuit. ‘He’d totally game-end her if he found her.’

‘She’s disappointed because her invention to combine our powers failed.’

'I'd be raging about that, too, it was a disaster.' I shook my head.

'And, most of all, I think she's lonely. As long as she's hiding from McMonaghan and living with a secret identity, she can't have any friends, or speak to her family. I bet she misses them.'

As much as I hated to admit it, that did make sense.

Miss Fortress came back into the room with a full cup, and I decided to take action.

'You know, Miss, my mum and nanny go to Zumba classes, so this investigation is important to me.'

'Ah,' she said. 'I can understand that. You need to look for connections – what do all of the victims have in common?'

'So, there's the Zumba, obviously,' said Jess.

'Are they all in the same class?' Miss Fortress clung to her coffee cup like it was life.

'No, different classes, but all at the new leisure centre,' Jess said, not following my lead in spite of the looks I was giving her.

'You should start there, then,' Miss Fortress said.

'We could go with Mum and Nanny to their

class next time,' I said. 'Just to watch, obviously, and see what we can find out.' I side-eyed Miss Fortress. 'I wouldn't want anything to happen to them – I don't know what I'd do without my mum.'

'You spend half your life moaning about your mum,' Jess snorted.

'Well, mums can be so annoying,' I said. 'What's your mum like, Miss?'

'Over-protective, fusses too much, cooks me dinners that are far too big…' she sighed. 'I really miss her.'

'When was the last time you saw her?' Jess said.

'I haven't been home to Singapore for six years,' Miss Fortress said. 'When I met Montgomery McMonaghan and we started working together on ways of enhancing the human brain, we were totally engrossed in our research and each other. We lived in a wonderful bubble. I Skyped my mum, of course, and my brother and sister, but I wish I'd taken the time to visit.'

She took a massive gulp of coffee.

'What about friends?' I said. 'Who did you hang out with when you weren't working?'

'Only each other,' Miss Fortress said.

'Didn't Montgomery McMonaghan have any friends or family?'

'He had a mother and father, but he was an only child. He used to visit his mother once a week – they were very close – but his relationship with his father was more complicated, so he waited until his dad was out of the house before visiting.'

'Didn't you ever go with him?' Jess said.

'No, I sensed that he'd rather go alone. His time with his mother was precious to him. And when she passed away, that's when he started to change.'

'Why didn't you go home to your family?' I said.

'By the time I realised that he wanted to use our research to do unspeakably evil things, it was far too dangerous. I knew he'd be desperate to find me and that my home was the first place he'd look. Going there would put me and my family in danger. My only option was to disappear without saying a word to them. My poor mum doesn't know if I'm dead or alive.'

An actual tear spilled out of the corner of her eye. She quickly wiped it away with her sleeve, but it was an awful sight. Imagine your teacher crying – nobody wants to see that.

'How long ago was that?' Jess said.

'Almost two years ago now.'

'You haven't spoken to anyone who knows you in two years?' I said. 'That's awful! What do you do at home?'

'I scan the police radio frequencies to listen out for anything suspicious. I recognise all the different officers' voices now, so it's almost like I know them.'

'Ooh, anything exciting?' I said.

'Just a spate of burglaries, and they're keeping an eye on a released convict who's just returned to the area. Also, I think there's something romantic going on between two of the officers who I have given the names Jack and Rose.' Her face got all excited.

'You must be really lonely, Miss,' I said.

'Other than Monty, there was only one person in this country that I really cared about, and I had to...'

She turned her head so we couldn't see her face, but her shoulders were shaking like she was properly crying. 'You'd better go,' she said. 'The bell will ring soon.'

'So what are we thinking?' I said, as we sat next to our best mate, Darth Daver, on the Reflection bench for the last five minutes of break.

'When's your mum's next Zumba class?' Jess said, trying to fix her scarf so that it covered every bit of her neck.

'Saturday morning, I think. Maybe we could go before our shift at the animal sanctuary.' We'd started helping at the sanctuary when we were investigating the weird animal disappearances and had stayed on after because it was actually really cool. It's also where I'd met Mr P, so I felt like I owed them. After Rex and his mum had helped all the animals from the SPARC animal experiment lab, the sanctuary had been given loads of donations. They had another full-time worker there, so they didn't need much help, but we still went in a couple of times a week.

'Yeah, let's do that,' Jess said. 'At least it will be warm in the leisure centre.'

'That's ages away, though,' I said.

'Alex, it's like tomorrow,' Jess huffed, and a puff of white steamed out of her nostrils.

'But we need to do more now. I don't want my mum or nanny turning into a zombie. And – I have no idea how yet – but I reckon Montgomery McMonaghan is involved in this somehow.'

'There's no evidence to suggest that, is there?' Dave (aka Darth Daver) said.

'No,' I said, 'but that's probably because we have no evidence at all. And remember Montgomery McMonaghan knows about us now. He recognised us at the lab when we got all the animals out of there. It's only a matter of time before he makes his move against us.'

We sat shivering in silence for a moment.

'Miss Fortress said to find the connections,' Jess said. 'What do we know about the Zumba teacher?'

'Can you hack the Zumba teacher, Dave?' I was starting to get excited.

'Considering we don't even know the Zumba teacher's name, I'm thinking that's one of the stupidest questions you've ever asked,' Jess said.

'But we could find out easily. I'll see if Mum or Nanny know.'

'Asking your nanny someone's name is going to make an exciting scene for your movie.'

'I'll throw in a few forward rolls and some martial arts moves,' I said. 'It'll be great.'

'Who's going to play you in the movie?' Dave said.

'I shall be playing myself, of course. I am a talented actor, as well as being an amazing secret agent.'

'And who will play...'

'Don't you dare ask him, Dave.' Jess gave him one of her most scary looks.

Dave looked back at her and smiled. '...Jess?'

Jess whacked him in the arm.

'I'm glad you asked, David,' I said. 'I've given this a great deal of thought and have come to the conclusion that no actor could possibly match Jess's death-stare ability, wildlife-enclosure hair or teeny-tiny stature. So Jess will have to be CGI'd in.'

Dave cracked up, while Jess gave him the stink-eye.

'We could get that guy who played Gollum in *The Lord of the Rings* to do the motion-capture stuff,' I added, enjoying the violent shade of bright pink that flooded Jess's cheeks.

5

Deeper Undercover Than We Wanted To Be

'Please, Mum,' I said. 'We'll be really good and not get in the way at all.'

'I just can't understand why you want to go,' Mum said, looking around for her car keys that I had hidden in the porch to buy us more time to win her over. 'You've never shown the slightest interest before.'

'I was interested,' I said, keeping a bit of distance so she wouldn't smell the fartiness coming out of my ear. 'But I was worried that going to Zumba would make me look weak and girlish.'

'Zumba is neither weak nor girlish,' Mum said, emptying her handbag on to the floor.

'I know that now. I was a victim of toxic masculinity spread by the media.' Jess had made me practise that part a lot.

'If that's true, Alex,' Mum said. 'Why do I think you just want to go so you can take the mick?'

'I'm hurt that you have such a low opinion of me, Mother,' I said, desperately trying to think of some way to change her mind.

'The truth is, Mrs Sparrow…' Jess jumped in, and I really hoped she knew where she was going with this '…since the situation with Mrs Spires, Alex has been worried about you and his nan going to Zumba class in case the same thing happens to you.'

My ear didn't fart and my mum stopped rummaging and gave me a squeeze. It was annoying that while my lies failed miserably, Jess's boring truth-telling saved the day.

'Oh, Alex, love,' she said. 'Nanny and I will be absolutely fine, I promise. But if you want to come and watch for reassurance, then I'll take you. If I ever find my keys.'

'I think I might have accidentally seen them in the porch, in Lauren's right ladybird welly, behind the big umbrella in the corner,' I said, sitting on the bottom stair to put my trainers on.

'Right,' Mum said, opening the porch door. 'Let's go then, shall we? We need to pick up Nanny on the way.'

Soon we were in the car outside Nanny's house. I got out and knocked for her while Mum and Jess waited in the car. Nanny was wearing tracksuit bottoms with purple stripes down the sides, and a matching hooded top. I was really glad she wasn't wearing tight leggings – it was bad enough seeing those on my mum.

'Alex, what are you doing here?' she said, leaning forward to give me a hug.

'I'm coming to Zumba to keep an eye on you, Nanny,' I said, knowing how adorable she found my cheekiness.

'Ooh, the others are going to be so jealous.' Her face lit up. 'I have the most handsome and thoughtful grandson in the world.'

The leisure centre was a massive grey building,

still new and shiny-looking because it only opened a couple of years ago. We had to walk up a long, winding ramp to the entrance, which was next to the outside swimming pool. It was brilliant in the summer when everyone from school was there, and we played giant games of swim-tag where we had to dive off the inflatables and hit each other with beach balls. But in the winter it looked like a scene out of an apocalyptic movie when the people are all gone, and packs of dogs roam the land, scavenging for human body parts.

'I would *love* to push you in there, Alex,' Jess said, looking at the pool a bit too longingly for my liking. I moved away from her and a bit closer to Nanny, who I knew would protect me if things turned bad.

'Can you imagine how cold it would be in there, right now?' Nanny said. 'I wouldn't swim in there for a million pounds and a date with Alan Titchmarsh.'

I tried not to think about that as the huge glass doors swished open, letting a whoosh of warmth on to my face.

'Two for Zumba, please,' my mum said to the lady

at the counter, who looked really bored and was trying to play games on her phone under the desk.

'What about the kids?' she said, glancing up at me and Jess.

'They're just watching,' Mum said.

'Can't let them through the barriers unless they have a pass,' said the lady, whose name badge said she was called Angel. 'So that's sixteen pounds for the four of you.' She printed out the tickets and Nanny took them, leaving Mum to scrape around in her purse for some cash.

'Come on, you two,' Nanny said. 'I'll take you to the studio.'

We followed Nanny through the turnstiles and down some stairs. To get to the studio we had to walk through a proper gym area, where people were doing stuff on all those machines like you see on TV and the movies. There were the ones people run on, and ones where people had to pull down on bars. One guy was lying on a bench, lifting up an enormous weight, with sweat dripping down the sides of his head. Everything smelt of exercise and rubber.

At the back of the gym, Nanny led us through a door that said 'Studio 3', and into a room with a wooden floor and mirrors covering one of the walls. At the front of the room was what I can only describe as a man-giant, with a glistening brown body made of pure muscle, a vest so tight it would have been too small for my little sister, and pulled-up sports socks whiter than Simon Cowell's teeth.

'We've come to the wrong studio, Nanny,' I said. 'This must be The Rock body-double club.'

'You can't look like that in here.' The man-giant was pointing at Jess.

'Oh, that's her normal face – she really can't help it,' I said.

'I mean the footwear,' man-giant said. 'I'm not feeling those boots for Zumba. You need something you can flex in.'

'I'm not dancing,' Jess said, turning red in the face.

'You guys paid for passes?'

Jess nodded, looking like she wanted to disappear into the floor.

'Then you are dancing, my friends.' He pinged the elastic on his shorts and took a swig from his drink bottle. 'But not in those. You need to get some kicks on, girl.'

'Da'Shon, this is my grandson, Alex, and his friend, Jess.' Nanny beamed, just as Mum walked into the studio, followed by a stream of other ladies.

'Alex and Jess,' Da'Shon said, 'you are most welcome here at Da'Shon's Diamond Zumba. Alex, you're fine in what you've got on. Can anyone lend Jess here some shoes so she can get her dance on?'

'She looks about my size,' a lady said. 'She can borrow my spares.' She handed Jess a pair of neon pink trainers. Jess looked at them in horror. 'Don't worry, duck, they've had odour eaters in them all week, so the smell should have gone by now.'

'Thanks, Eileen,' Da'Shon said. 'And welcome back, Rose – you gave us a bit of a scare but we should have known you'd be back, you tough old girl.'

Everyone laughed and clapped while Mrs Spires tutted and told Eileen that she didn't like her new hair.

'Alex.' Jess pulled me into a corner while the ladies chatted and took their coats off. 'I can't do this.'

'I know it's not the coolest,' I said. 'But no one from school is going to see us.'

'I mean it, Alex. I can't.'

'Listen, Jess, if this bunch of old ladies can do Zumba, it's got to be easier than catching a weedle on Pokemon Go.'

Jess looked like she was going to puke.

'Also, if we join in, we'll earn their trust, which will be better for the mission.'

She did a little swallow, which I'm pretty sure was because she'd vomited in her mouth.

'Look, we'll stay at the back, OK. Just do your best.' I patted her on the arm. 'Now change into Eileen's smelly trainers and let's get this done.'

Jess's eyes widened as she looked over my shoulder. 'Are you sure you want to be in the back?' she smirked.

'Why? What is it?' I said, turning around to see what she was staring at. 'Sweet balls of fudge,' I gasped, unable to look away from the horror in front of me. The Zumba ladies were all lined up, ready to start the class. Some of them wore tracksuit bottoms and T-shirts, but lots of them were in leggings and vests, with rainbow-coloured fitness bands on their wrists. Some of them were wearing crop tops. My *nanny* was wearing a crop top. I don't want to sound ageist but, honestly, who wants to see their nanny's bare stomach skin? Nobody, that's who. Goddamn nobody. And when the music started for the warm-up, things went from bad to full-on, end-of-the-world, disaster mode. There was jiggling, my friends. Lots and lots of jiggling.

'Come on, ladies, let's see that slide 'n' tap,' Da'Shon shouted from the front, while demonstrating with the vigour of an alpha tiger. There were about twenty ladies in the class, and one man, who must have been even older than my nanny. They started to dance.

I decided the best thing to do was to focus on Da'Shon and throw myself into the Zumba. So, as the music played, I shrugged in my head and started to slide and tap with them. Jess was on my left, swaying slightly, her feet barely leaving the floor. I guess she needed a bit of time to get into it.

'Now, let's get those arms swingin' in four, three, two...' Da'Shon swished his arms with a swag that made me jealous, and the rest of the class copied. Then he added in a spin and some extra footwork and everyone followed without missing a step. In the corner of my eye, I could see my mum in the second row. I hated to say it but she was actually quite good. I glanced over at Jess again, and she was sort of shuffling around, tripping over herself, and flapping her hands a bit. It was hilarious.

At the end of the song, we all stopped for a few seconds, and everyone smiled around at each other and took a swig of water.

'Nice warm-up.' Da'Shon clapped his hands. 'And now on to the juicy part. As you all know, Zumba groups across London are planning a joint world record-breaking attempt for the biggest flash Zumba dance ever.'

Everyone started chatting, like they were dead excited.

'I have just had the ping,' Da'Shon said. 'The flash is going to take place here in Cherry Tree Lane within the next two weeks.'

There were gasps around the room.

'So, we have got to get learning that routine,' Da'Shon said, and everyone cheered. 'I'm gonna be working you hard, so I don't wanna hear no complaining, and I don't wanna hear no crying. I'm looking at you, Alan.'

Everyone laughed and Alan pretended to get a tissue out of his pocket and rub his eyes.

Part of me thought that I should be thinking about how embarrassing the whole thing was. But a bigger part of me was thinking that it was actually quite fun and funny and that I had a warm feeling in my heart. Probably because it was Christmas.

'We are going to be dancing our tushies off to *All I Want for Christmas is You* by the diva that is Mariah Carey,' Da'Shon said. 'It's a Christmas classic and we are going to do it the justice it deserves. Here we go, and you newbies in the back, do your best to keep up.'

So then we started to learn the routine. Now I'm not one for making excuses, as you know, but I have to point out that it's a fast song, and I'm an inexperienced Zumba-er, and I was trying to keep an eye on Mrs Spires, who was picking up the routine faster than anyone else in the class. Fifteen minutes later and I was dripping with sweat.

'Jess,' I hissed. 'Do you know when we get a break?'

'I don't think we do,' Jess said.

'But I'm dying.'

'Really?' Jess sniggered. 'All the old ladies look OK.'

I looked around the room. At Mum. At Nanny. At Mrs Spires. They were hardly even sweating. 'How is that possible?'

'Not as easy as you thought, then?' Jess said.

'At least I'm actually dancing,' I said, 'and not just wobbling around like a sleep-walking penguin.' I'd looked over at her quite a few times and Jess was literally the world's worst dancer.

'Here we go,' Da'Shon clapped. 'Let's take it from the top, and I want to see a lot more hip action in the chorus.'

'Ugh,' I said. 'I think I've seen enough hip action. I'm going to have to cut out my eyeballs.'

Jess nearly choked as a laugh spluttered out of her mouth. 'Your nan puts a lot of enthusiasm into her pelvic thrusts.'

'Stop it,' I said. 'I'm not even listening right now.' And I started the routine again with everyone else.

'Give me a whoop-whoop!' Da'Shon said, and everyone started joyfully whooping. I may have let out a small whoop myself.

'Eileen, you are on point today. Now give me the Da'Shon shimmy.' Da'Shon started shaking his shoulders, and I watched him closely rather than looking at the jiggling again.

Everything was going great, and then Eileen, who was in the row in front of me, suddenly stumbled. At first I thought she'd tripped, but she fell to the ground fast and heavy, with a horrid thump. I couldn't hear it because the music was so loud, but I felt it through the floor. It made my heart lurch in my chest.

We all rushed over to her, as the music cut into silence.

'Not again,' someone said.

'Stand back,' Da'Shon said, pushing through the crowd. 'Someone call an ambulance.'

'OMG, Jess,' I whispered, looking at Eileen who just seconds ago had been twerking with the energy of someone half her age, but was now lying lifeless on the floor. 'They're dropping faster than stormtroopers in a blaster battle.'

6

Da'Lies

'Get the defibrillator,' Da'Shon said, while keeping two fingers on Eileen's neck to check her pulse and his ear to her face to see if she was breathing.

My mum darted out of the room.

'Who's The Defibrillator?' I whispered to Jess. 'And how is he going to help?'

'It's not a person, idiot,' she said. 'It's one of those machines that electric shocks people's hearts to start them back up.'

'Oh, man,' I said. 'Is Eileen going to die?'

Jess didn't say anything.

Mum ran in with a silver case, putting it on the floor next to Da'Shon and lifting the clip to open it. Inside was some fancy equipment with wires and a monitor and two flat paddles with handles to hold them. It was like what you see on hospital dramas on the TV where they say, 'Charging to two hundred. Clear.' I felt sick.

But then, for no apparent reason, Eileen jolted and opened her eyes.

'I thought they had to put the paddles on her chest for it to work,' I said.

'They do,' Jess frowned. 'How did she get that shock when nothing was touching her?'

Eileen sat up, looking a bit confused. 'They've had odour eaters in them all week,' she said.

'Lie down, Eileen,' Nanny Sparrow said. 'You've had a turn.'

They all laid Eileen back down on the floor, with folded-up coats under her head and draped over her to keep her warm. She seemed weirdly fine, arguing with everyone, saying she wanted to get up and back to the routine. By the time the paramedics arrived, she was laughing and joking about the fuss she'd caused and insisting that she'd never felt better. They took her to hospital anyway, just to check her over.

'So our time's nearly up for today,' Da'Shon said, once the paramedics had carried Eileen out on a stretcher and into the waiting ambulance. 'Let's get back on it next week. And, in the meantime, I want you all to stick to the healthy lifestyle schedules I drew up for you. It's important.' He looked around at everyone in the group. 'Make sure you follow them exactly, including the meal plans.'

Alan let out a little groan.

Da'Shon stared at Alan with the intensity of Kylo Ren trying to read someone's mind. 'I mean it, Alan. No messing.'

It seemed a bit over the top. Jess and me gave each other a look.

'For those of you who have signed up to Da'Shon's Daily Dinners, I will see you this afternoon with some deliciously healthy grub. For those of you who haven't signed up yet – I strongly suggest you do so A-sap.'

There was something about the way he said it – such a change from the lighthearted way he'd spoken throughout the class. I needed to ask him some questions.

'Da-Shon,' I said, as he turned to start packing up the defibrillator.

'Hold on, Alex, I need to take this back to reception.'

I could see Mrs Spires looking at it like it was the last cake in a shop, but Angel appeared in the doorway and took it before Mrs Spires could pounce. As she grabbed the handle, I noticed she had a tiny tattoo on the inside of one of her fingers.

'Now what can I do for you, my friend?' Da'Shon said.

'I wanted to know more about your Daily Dinners,' I said. 'I was wondering if I should sign up.'

'I think that would have to be your mum's decision,' said Da'Shon. 'And she's already told me that she cooks healthy meals at home. I tried to persuade her, but she said she loves to cook.'

'What's so special about them?' I asked, as innocently as possible.

'Homemade food, calorie-counted, fresh organic ingredients,' he said.

'And that's all?' I said

'That's all,' he nodded. And as he did, I felt a

rumbling erupt in my ear. Jess was crouching on the floor, taking off Eileen's trainers. She sniffed and looked up.

'Do you cook all the food yourself?' I said.

'With my own two hands here in the leisure-centre kitchens,' he said. 'I'm not just a pretty face.'

I really liked Da'Shon. I didn't want there to be something sinister about him, but as he picked up his sports bag and left, I had a horrible feeling.

'Do you think he's putting something bad in the food?' Jess said.

'He's definitely hiding something. And it's too much of a coincidence that people in his Zumba classes keep almost dying. We need to find out more about Da'Shon.'

'And we need to see how he makes the dinners.'

'Agent Bob?' I said.

'Agent Bob,' Jess nodded.

Jess came to my house after our shift at the animal sanctuary so that we could work together on Bob. He'd been out on a lot of missions over the past couple of months – we literally couldn't have managed without him. Unfortunately, the last time he'd helped us, he'd ended up in a muddy puddle.

It made him sick for days. We knew it would take a lot to get him out of the shiny new tank he shared with Elle, and back into danger.

We stood at the breakfast bar close, but not too close, to the tank. Bob didn't like it when we steamed up his walls with our 'bacteria-infested human breath'.

'We have a job we'd like you to help us with, Bob,' Jess said.

'Minimal risk,' I said.

'We'd need to put you in your jar, which we will clean thoroughly, of course, and hide you in a kitchen in the leisure centre.'

'Minimal risk,' I said.

'We just want you to watch someone...'

'The target,' I interrupted, annoyed that Jess wasn't using the correct spy words.

'We want you to watch...' Jess made an 'I'm-refusing-to-use-your-stupid-word' face, '...*him*, make some dinners. We need to know what ingredients he's using, and if he's doing anything suspicious with the food.'

'Minimal risk,' I said.

'We're willing to pay,' Jess said. 'Though we're a bit low on money since buying your new tank, we're open to requests and will do our best to get you what you want.'

'Did I mention, minimal risk?'

Jess twitched, then looked up, surprised. 'He'll do it.'

'What?' I looked at Bob in his tank. He'd stopped swimming his circuits and was staring right at us, his orange scales glistening. It might have been my imagination, but I swear he looked less plump and more muscular than he had a few months ago. I guess with everything that had happened, he was changing. I wasn't just looking at a goldfish, I was looking at a primed and ready member of our agent team, at the peak of his physical and mental abilities. I could see Elle looking over at him from her favourite spot by the coral.

'Bob,' I whispered. 'Elle is making proper heart-eyes at you.'

At that, Elle darted into the coral and Bob went back to swimming his circuits.

'You know she can hear you too, right?' Jess said. 'She's like twenty centimetres away. Talk about ruining a moment.'

'Sorry,' I said. 'My bad. Now, let's leave these

lovefish to it and put together a dossier on Da'Shon.' I grabbed a bit of paper from the recycling pile that my dad had spilt his coffee on. 'Perfect. A proper dossier must have a coffee stain.'

'A dossier?' Jess raised her eyebrows.

'It's the official name for it, Jessticles, and, as you know, I am a top, professional agent.'

'So what do we know about Da'Shon? Do we even know his last name?'

'Hold on, I'll ask Mum,' I said, jumping off my stool. 'No, scrap that, Mum will think I'm up to something and asking too many questions. I'll ask Nanny – she'll never suspect me.'

I ran into the lounge, where Nanny was watching a quiz show.

'Nanny, what is Da'Shon's last name?'

'It's Darola,' she said, smiling at me. 'Isn't it brilliant – Da'Shon Darola – who'd have thought a name like that could exist?'

'Yeah, it is quite swag,' I said, wondering if there was any way I could make Alex Sparrow sound cooler.

'How long has he been your Zumba teacher for?' I said.

'Just a few months,' Nanny said. 'Our old teacher left suddenly and Da'Shon replaced her. Although none of us were complaining, he's given us a new lease of life.'

My agent alert was tingling hard. This was all a bit convenient – almost like it had been set up.

'Do you know where he worked before that?' I asked.

'I assume at another fitness centre somewhere. Why do you want to know, darling?'

'Um, I'm writing something about inspirational people for school,' I said, my ear growling. 'I chose you and Da'Shon.'

'Well, that's nice,' she said. 'Let me know if you need any help.'

'I will, thanks, Nanny.'

I ran back into the kitchen and made Jess write down everything we knew, then we briefed Bob on the plan.

'Da'Shon makes the dinners every day,' Jess said. 'So we'll plant you in the kitchen tomorrow morning, and collect you when he leaves to make his deliveries.'

'Easy.' I shrugged. 'What could go wrong?'

7

Finding the Fat

The next morning, I woke up and thought I'd been run over in my sleep. Every single part of my body was throbbing. Mum seemed annoyingly fine, and my secret respect for the old ladies in the Zumba class grew a touch bigger. Jess's mum dropped her at my house so we could go to the leisure centre together and execute the plan. Dave had emailed us a map of the centre. Not the standard one you could find on the website – a more detailed one which included all the staff-only areas.

'You know you can't ever break up with Dave,' I said. 'Because I don't think we could do this without him.'

'Shut up, Alex. Let's go so we can get Bob in place before it gets too busy.'

'Mum,' I called. 'Can me and Jess go to the leisure centre?'

Mum walked into the kitchen. 'Have you finished your homework?'

'Technically no,' I said. 'But my health should come first, right?'

'You did a whole Zumba class yesterday.'

'That's not enough, though. I need to be exercising as much as possible. You wouldn't want me to get ill and die, would you?'

'Of course not, love, and I'm glad you're taking your health seriously all of a sudden. Even though you've never seemed the slightest bit bothered about it before.'

'I'm going to be healthy all the time now, Mum. It's my new thing.' I gave her my most truthful face. 'Now, just let me grab some crisps and you can give us a lift to the leisure centre.'

'Don't you want to walk?' Mum said.

'It's like ten minutes away, and I can't be bothered.'

Five minutes later, we were walking up the ramp to the centre, the freezing wind whipping our scarves into our faces and penetrating even the thickest parts of my puffy coat. We'd wrapped Bob's jar in a fleecy princess blanket that I'd stolen from Lauren's bed.

'What would happen if the water in Bob's jar froze?' I said. 'Do you think he'd be cryogenically frozen? Then he could be revived in the future, when it's possible to combine fish and humans, to make a super-race of merpeople.'

'Let's just concentrate on getting him in and out of the kitchen without him ending up as someone's lunch, shall we?'

'Affirmative.' I approached Angel at the counter. 'Two of your finest passes, please.'

'Passes for what?'

'Passes for what?' I asked Jess. I hadn't thought I'd need to be specific.

'Swimming, please,' she said.

'Four pounds each.'

I pulled some money out of my wallet and reluctantly handed it over. As Angel took it, I got a better look at her tattoo – it was a tiny black octopus.

'Cool,' I said, leaning forward to get a better look. Angel quickly pulled her hand back.

We found a quietish place, behind a big room where a karate lesson was taking place. Jess unzipped the bag.

'Are you OK, Bob?' she whispered, twitching as he responded and then looking at me in surprise.

'He wants something from us,' she said.

'I should have known it was too easy. What does he want? I literally have two pounds right now.'

'He wants to talk.'

'To talk? About what?'

Jess juddered around a bit. 'Matters of the heart,' she said. 'We need somewhere more private.'

We made our way down the main staircase and along the long corridor past the gym, with the swimming-pool smell getting stronger until we reached the family changing rooms. It was pretty busy, but that was good in a way because there was a lot of noise cover and nobody really paying us any attention. We found two free cubicles next to each other in the far corner of the room. Jess took Bob into one, and I locked myself into the pod next door.

'Oh man, my seat's wet,' I said, looking at the watery patch on the bench that meant I couldn't sit down without getting a soggy bottom.

'Shut up, Alex. Bob needs to talk to us.'

'Is your seat wet, though?'

'No, nice and dry and comfy,' Jess said, and I swear I could hear her snuggling her bottom into the plastic bench.

'Can we swap?' I said.

'No chance.' She snorted.

'My whole body aches from Zumba.'

'Mine too.'

'But you hardly moved through the whole class, how can you possibly be aching? I was working out like a bad-A.'

'I moved a lot!' Her voice went a bit high and annoyed.

'You were like a slug with a limp, Jess.' I leaned against the side of the cubicle next to Jess and Bob. 'So, what's on your mind, Bob?'

There was a minute of mostly silence, but with a few squeaks as Jess's twitching made her slide a little on the bench.

'OK. Bob and Elle are thinking about starting a family. It's a big step, and Elle has told Bob that she wants to be sure he understands what it will mean, before they take the plunge.'

'Jeez – you're having kids?!' I spluttered.

'They're discussing it,' Jess said. 'Bob used to think of himself as a solitary being, like an octopus…'

'Speaking of,' I interrupted, 'did you see Angel's tattoo? We can tick another thing off the awesome movie list.'

'Doesn't count,' Jess huffed. 'And getting back to the point, things have changed for Bob now. He never knew his family – the only family he's ever spent any time with is yours…'

'I can hear, even through this moist plastic wall, that you have thoughts on my family, Jess.'

'It's just that all families are different, aren't they?'

'Yeah, so?'

'So, Bob watching how your family works might not give him the full picture.'

'Meaning?'

'Like the way you speak to your mum. She's really kind and you're rude to her all the time.'

'That's just our vibe.'

'And you always use your nan to get your own way.'

'Err, that's what nannies are for.'

'And you have zero respect for your sister,' Jess said.

'She's the most annoying person in the world. What's your point?'

'My point is that if Bob needs to understand what family means, he's going to need to do more than observe the Sparrows.'

'I suppose your family is perfect then, is it? With your dad not living with you and your mum working at weird times of day.'

'I see my dad lots, and Mum helps people in trouble. Sometimes that happens at the weekends or at night, but I'm glad that she does it.'

'Sucks for you when she misses your things, though, doesn't it?'

'Why do you have to be so…? Hold on, Bob's talking.'

Jess was quiet for a moment, which was probably a good thing because it gave me a chance to stop hulking out. She made me so mad sometimes.

'Bob says we're not helping,' Jess sighed. 'And that if we can't tell him anything useful, he's not going on the mission for us.'

'I guess we're not,' I said. 'Sorry, Jess. Sorry, Bob.'

'I'm sorry, too,' Jess said. 'What is family? It's a hard question to answer.'

'Oh!' I jumped and whacked my elbow on the cubicle. 'I know the answer! It's "family means nobody gets left behind or forgotten".'

'You got that from *Lilo and Stitch*!' I could hear Jess rolling her eyes.

'Maybe. It's true, though, isn't it?'

'It's a start, I suppose,' Jess said. 'But I think Bob wants more.'

'Can we work on it and get back to you, Bob?' I said.

'He agrees.'

'Right then, let's get this mission on the road.' I swung open the door to my cubicle in a dramatic and meaningful way, which was ruined a bit when I slipped as I stepped out. 'We have an evil kitchen to infiltrate.'

With Bob safely tucked away, we walked towards the changing-room door and Jess whispered, 'Isn't that Mrs Spires?'

I looked up to see Mrs Spires over by the ledge where people plug their hairdryers and mobile phone chargers in. She was sitting on it, leaning against the mirror, surrounded by people drying their hair. As we got closer, I saw that there was a wire coming out of her fitness band, which was still on her wrist, and that it was plugged into one of the sockets. She must have been charging it. When a lady nearby put her dryer down to get something out of her bag, Mrs Spires grabbed it and hugged it really tight into her body.

'We should talk to her,' I said, trying to seem brave and not at all freaked out by Mrs Spires.

Jess nodded.

I walked over with the confidence of Thanos wearing the infinity gauntlet. 'Hi, Mrs Spires,' I shouted so she could hear me over the hairdrying noise.

'Oh, it's you two,' she said. She seemed as happy to see us as always.

'So, Zumba was eventful yesterday,' I said.

'I heard Mamie had a turn,' Mrs Spires said.

'Yeah, we heard that, too,' I said. I almost said 'from you' but I decided it wouldn't help the situation if she got annoyed with me.

'And Eileen, yesterday,' Jess added.

‘Terrible,’ Mrs Spires said. ‘Still, she’s fine, so no harm done.’

‘Are you alright, Mrs Spires?’ I had to ask. She was clearly not alright, but I wanted to know if she believed that she was.

‘I’ve never felt better,’ she said. She wasn’t lying.

‘Do you know what made you collapse?’ Jess said. I gave her an annoyed look – it was my job to ask the questions.

‘Not yet. I have a check-up with the doctor on Friday morning,’ Mrs Spires said. ‘Should find out more then, not that it’s any of your business.’

The lady whose hairdryer Mrs Spires was cradling like a baby had stood up again and was looking a bit irritated.

‘I think that lady wants her hairdryer back,’ I said.

Mrs Spires handed it over, pulled the charging lead out of her wrist band, and jumped down off the ledge. Quite energetically, actually. ‘I’m on my way out now anyway.’ And she half bounced, half danced away towards the stairs.

‘Well, this isn’t getting any less weird,’ Jess sighed. ‘Let’s get Bob into the kitchen and have some lunch.’

Using Dave's brilliant map, it was easy to find the centre's kitchens on the main floor behind the coffee bar. He'd also managed to print us out a copy of the staff rota, so we knew exactly how many staff were in the building and where they were supposed to be. Angel was on reception with Simon. Kevin and Raksha were running Toddler World on the bottom floor. Destiny was on the main floor, ready to supervise a birthday swimming party, and Andy, Jamaal and Matilda were on lifeguard duty at the pool. Amani was working at the coffee bar. Heather, Jaz and Dilesh were personal training in the gym. Fi was holding a yoga class and Sensei Dominic was teaching karate. We waited until there were massive queues at the front desk, with a whole birthday party of four year olds running around screaming, so that the only floating staff member, Giles, had to help out, and then we slipped through the door marked 'STAFF ONLY'. Those were my favourite kind of doors, second only to ones marked 'PRIVATE' and 'NO ENTRY'.

I crept towards the kitchen on my stealthiest tiptoes, ducking and diving every now and then.

'Are you humming the *Mission Impossible*

theme?' Jess asked. 'And why are you walking so weirdly?'

'Shush, Jessticles – and be careful of the lasers.'

'Listen, Double-O-Dum-Dum,' Jess said. 'We know our path is clear to the kitchen but we don't know for how long. We need to be quick.'

'Oh, you're actually right, for a change. Speed over stealth.'

'Speed over singing,' Jess said.

I sprinted ahead. 'Hurry up, then!' I reached the door first and pushed it open. The inside of the kitchen was mostly shiny metal, like Taran's evil lab, but with cocktail sausages and cheesy puffs in bowls, and plates of cupcakes everywhere, instead of instruments of torture.

'I guess this is all for the party,' I said. 'So we'd better not hide Bob behind it in case it gets moved.'

Luckily, there were shelves full of cooking ingredients in bottles, jars and tubs. 'Where's a good spot for Bob?'

'We need to choose something that Da'Shon definitely won't be using in his healthy dinners,' Jess said.

'OK, if it looks disgusting, it's a no-go,' I said, skimming the shelf. 'Find a can of something delicious and we'll stick Bob behind that. What the heck is quinoa?'

'Don't put him near the quinoa,' Jess said. 'Or the cous-cous.'

'Why does everything here have a weird name?' I said. 'Edamame?'

'Pass,' Jess said. 'And avoid anything that has the word "artisan" on the label.'

'Chia?'

'Skip it.'

'Goji?'

'No.'

'Peanut butter?'

'Organic?'

I picked up the giant jar and read the ingredients. 'No, made with palm oil and sugar.'

'That's the one,' Jess said. 'Oh look, and it's next to the Nutella. This is perfect.'

We snuggled Bob in behind the peanut butter and Nutella, wished him luck and then left the kitchen.

'You know, we should really think up our own special good luck phrase for the movie. Like "May the force be with you" but something that relates specifically to us.'

'We really shouldn't,' Jess said.

'I know it's hard to beat "May the force be with you",' I said. 'But that doesn't mean we shouldn't try. How about "May the stink be with you"?'

'Rubbish.'

'I'll take that as a yes,' I said.

'Let's just go have our sandwiches,' Jess sighed.

'OK,' I said. 'And Jess?'

'What?'

'May the stink be with you.'

We had to spend the whole day in the leisure centre, doing everything we could think of to fill the time, other than exercise. It was so boring, it was almost painful. We watched Da'Shon enter the building at 14:06 and sign in at the main desk while flirting with Angel. We watched him being friendly to everyone he passed, high-fiving kids and sharing in-jokes with the people that worked there. Basically, he put a smile on the face of everyone he met. I *really* didn't want him to be a bad guy.

At 16:18, he left the staff-only area with a stack of boxes and exited the building, heading for the car park. The sun had gone down and the car park was lit by streetlights, making it seem much later than it actually was. The boxes steamed in the cold air and Da'Shon risked dropping them by using one of his hands to pull his hood up. In the warm, bright leisure centre, slow Christmas music was playing, making me feel kind of happy and sad at the same time. Me and Jess watched Da'Shon through the window. He made his way to his car, opened the boot, and piled the boxes in. He looked kind of lonely.

'Why does it feel wrong to be spying on him?' I said. 'I usually live for this stuff.'

'Oh wow – are you actually getting a conscience about violating people's privacy?' Jess said. 'It's a Christmas miracle.'

'I'm not proud of it, Jess. No need to rub it in.'

'Look, let's remember why we're doing this,' she said. 'To keep people safe.'

'You're right,' I sighed. 'Let's head back to the kitchen. I really want to get Bob and go home.'

It wasn't until after dinner that we had the chance to get Bob back in his tank and ask him what he'd seen. Elle was waiting for him, and they touched noses, which I think was a fish kiss. He swam a few circuits and had some food, and then he was ready to talk.

'So, what happened in the kitchen, Bob?' I said.

Jess sat twitching on her stool at the breakfast bar, occasionally stopping to ask quick questions, like, 'What then?' 'How much?' 'Could you see the label?' and 'Was it avocado?'

I waited impatiently, as always.

'Well?' I said, when Jess finished twitching.

'Bob said Da'Shon entered the kitchen, put his reusable supermarket bags on one of the counters, then took his coat off and plugged his phone in before putting on some upbeat music, some of which involved rap.'

'Good to know,' I said. Bob liked to notice every detail.

'Then he emptied the bags, which contained various fresh ingredients: skinless chicken breasts, kale, tomatoes, fennel, parsley...'

'It's OK, I get the picture,' I said. 'If it's OK with Bob, can we skip the rest of the list?'

Bob huffed in his tank and a little spray of bubbles shot up through the water.

'Using the ingredients from the bags and some from the shelves, including the edamame and quinoa, Da'Shon proceeded to cook large quantities of food while displaying an array of dance moves, such as the electric slide, the dab and the floss.'

'Nice,' I said.

'It all seemed wholesome and pleasant until about ten minutes before the food was ready to decant into the containers.'

'What happened?' I gasped.

'Get this,' Jess said. 'Da'Shon walked to the kitchen door, opened it and looked around, then returned to the counter. He opened his sports bag and removed several unlabelled small pots, then tipped whatever was in them into the food.'

'What the fudge was in those pots?' I said.

'And why did Da'Shon check that the coast was clear before putting them in the food?' said Jess.

'He didn't want anyone to see him,' I sighed. Usually these revelations made me super-happy, but this time I was disappointed. 'I really didn't want Da'Shon to be a bad guy,' I said. 'But he's obviously up to something.'

'I learnt with Taran that people who seem nice can be the opposite,' Jess said. 'But this sucks.'

We sat in silence for a couple of minutes.

'So we need to find out exactly what he's putting in the food,' I said.

'And if it's what's making the Zumba ladies collapse.'

'Oh, and if it's why Mrs Spires is acting so weird.' I took my hat off and raked my fingers through my hair. 'Because that is super-creepy.'

We thought in silence for a moment.

'And how is all of this linked to Montgomery McMonaghan?' I said.

'We have no reason to think that it is,' Jess said. 'Let's just concentrate on stopping anyone else almost dying.'

'Especially Mum and Nanny. I couldn't stand it if something happened to them. Mum is…'

'Alex!' Mum called from the lounge. 'We're walking Lauren across to The Pines – she wants to see the Christmas lights. Get your coat on.'

'So flipping annoying,' I stomped. 'I'm tired!' I yelled back. 'Why do I have to go?'

'It'll only take ten minutes, my sweet, and we go together every year. Jess can come too.'

'Fine,' I shouted. Even though it was absolutely, definitely not fine. 'But only for a minute.'

'Who are you trying to kid, Alex? You love The

Pines – you've been on about it for weeks. Once you get there you won't ever want to leave.' Jess snorted.

'Shut up, Jess, and get your coat,' I said, my rage already being replaced with excitement. The Pines was the best place in town over Christmas, and I needed a break from stressing over the looming Zumba disaster.

8

The Pines

The Pines was a tiny road near where I lived – one of those that doesn't lead anywhere, just curves round in a circle. The houses down The Pines were all big, detached and lux, and the people who lived in them drove fancy cars, like Mercedes and Jaguars. Even their wheelie bins seemed posher than everyone else's. I'd never been in any of the houses, but every Christmas I walked down The Pines a bunch of times, just to look at them. People who lived down The Pines made it their business to make it the most Christmassy, lit-up, magical place in Cherry Tree Lane.

We crossed the road outside my house and walked down the street. The pavement was narrow, so we mostly had to walk single file. Dad went first, then Mum, holding hands with Lauren, then Nanny, then me and Jess.

'So this is like a family tradition?' Jess said.

'Yeah, I guess,' I said. 'But with extra people this year.'

'You've got Mr Prickles in your coat, haven't you?'

I felt his nose tickling against my neck. His spikes didn't hurt too much because I'd put on a really thick jumper. 'He wanted to see the lights. Besides, he's part of the family.'

'You should have brought Bob and Elle, too,' Jess said.

'One step ahead of you, Jessticles, as always. Look after this, would you?' I handed Jess Bob and Elle in a jar.

'Blimey, Alex,' Jess said.

'We're supposed to be teaching him about family, aren't we?' I said. 'Part of family is doing stuff like this.' I didn't say it out loud but I felt glad that Jess was with us, too.

'Look at Mrs Spires' house,' I whispered as we walked past. It was shining brightly, the light on in every room, along with her Christmas lights, plus the radio and a couple of TVs from the sound of it. 'It's like a party house but with just Mrs Spires in there.'

'And Snuffles,' Jess said, pointing at his grumpy little face peering out of one of the upstairs windows.

We turned the corner on to Oak Avenue, which was mostly dark and quiet, apart from one house that, like Mrs Spires', was loud and lit up.

'Another party house,' I said. 'That's weird.'

'I bet it's another Zumba lady,' Jess said.

'Do you know who lives there, Nanny?' I called over to her.

'Oh yes, that's Alan's house. Although goodness knows what he's doing in there, making all that noise.'

We carried on down Oak, then turned on to Cherry Tree Lane until we reached The Pines. As we turned, we all slowed right down and said, 'Ooh.'

'It's even better than last year!' Mum said, gazing around at the houses.

Dad looked up from his phone. 'Wow,' he said. 'That's spectacular.'

'Can we do this to our house, Daddy?' Lauren asked, her cheeks all pink from the cold and the lights shining in her eyes.

'Err, maybe one day,' Dad said.

'Your daddy has a very important job and is extremely busy,' Nanny said proudly.

'But we could probably make a bit more effort with our house,' said Mum.

'You're going to buy the lights, are you?' Dad said. 'And climb ladders to put them up, and then take them all down at the end of Christmas?'

'I was just saying,' Mum said, 'that we could do a bit more. For the kids.'

'But it will be me that has to do it all,' Dad moaned. 'And think of the electricity bill. Are the kids going to pay it out of their pocket money?'

'Yes!' shouted Lauren, at the same time as I shouted, 'No!'

'Lauren can pay for it if she wants to,' I said. 'I'm not spending my hard-earned cash on the electricity bill.'

'But if we both pay, we can get more.' Lauren stamped her foot.

'And "hard-earned" is a bit of a stretch,' said Dad. 'You've hardly done any of your jobs lately.'

'I have, too!' I said, my ear farting loudly and stinkily.

'To be fair, Alex, you have let them slide a bit,' Mum said.

'He's in his last year of primary school,' Nanny said. 'He should be enjoying himself, not worrying about chores.'

'Thank you, Nanny,' I said.

'You always spoil him, Mum,' Dad said. 'He needs to take more responsibility.'

Of all the infuriating things to say, that had to be the worst considering everything I'd done the past few months, saving millions of people and animals and not even getting any credit for it. Of course, he didn't know that, but it wasn't the point. I opened my mouth to argue.

'Everybody!' Jess said. 'Look how beautiful it is.'

We'd reached the curve of the road without even noticing.

We all stopped and looked. The whole street was decorated like a scene from a movie. The houses and trees were covered in lights, some white, some multi-coloured. There were scenes laid out on the lawns: of snowmen and Christmas trees, of Santa and his reindeer; of polar bears and penguins and candy canes and elves. Lots of the statues were animatronic, so they moved and danced. Some of the houses had machines that puffed out fake snow, and some had holograms lighting up the whole side of their houses with festive greetings. It was a flipping wonderland.

For a moment there was silence. I pulled the zip of my coat down a bit, so Mr Prickles could see, and Jess did the same with Bob and Elle.

Someone in one of the houses started playing 'Fairytale of New York' on the piano, the notes drifting out to the street with a flurry of fake snow being puffed out of funnels dotted around the street, like droplets of coffee froth, and it was just perfect.

Dad put his arm around Mum; Lauren cuddled into Nanny; and me, Jess, Mr Prickles, Bob and Elle huddled together, taking it all in.

'We need to keep everyone safe,' I said. And I didn't just mean the people standing together on The Pines right then, although they were the most important people in the world to me. I meant Mrs Spires, and Eileen, and Mamie, Darth Daver and the kids at school, the animals at the rescue centre, the people who lived in these fancy houses and everyone in our town. I meant poor Miss Fortress, who hadn't seen her family for years and was totally alone.

Jess nodded. 'Whatever it takes.'

'OMG, can I just say: Perfect. Movie. Moment.'

'Why do you have to ruin everything?' Jess groaned.

'It's one of my many skills.' I took a bow.

'Ruining things is not a skill,' Jess said, as we finished walking The Pines and headed for home.

'Oh, Jessticles.' I shook my head. 'One day you will learn, my Padawan. One day. Now let's get back and make a plan.'

9

Soup and Salmon

'So what exactly is he putting in the food?' Miss Fortress said, pulling on a pair of mittens.

'We don't know,' Jess said.

'We were thinking we could steal his bag and send his pots to the lab,' I said. 'Aka to you.'

'But it would be really risky, so we thought it was worth asking you first.'

'You want me to steal his bag?' Miss Fortress blinked at us. 'If I'm going to have to start doing the dirty work myself, then why did I gift you two with such incredible powers?'

'Woah, Jess.' I reached a hand out to pull her back, knowing that she'd be over the desk in a fury within half a second. 'Firstly, Miss, we didn't mean for you to steal Da'Shon's bag, we wanted to ask you whether anything in the food could affect the ladies in the way we told you about.'

Jess was staring at Miss Fortress and grinding her teeth like a cave-woman about to slaughter a mammoth.

'And second, we do plenty of dirty work, you didn't "gift" us the powers, and they're not that incredible. Well, they're great and everything, but...'

'They hardly make us Superman,' Jess said.

'Speak for yourself, Jess.' But I whispered because I didn't want to make her even crosser.

'Right. Right. I'm sorry, I'm just...' Miss Fortress pulled a bobble hat over her head. Her hair was in a high bun, so the hat didn't go on properly and made her head look a freakish shape. 'To know if the food is affecting the victims, I'd really need to see medical notes – blood tests, ECGs, that sort of thing.'

'You want blood, we'll get blood.' I jumped up, feeling excited by the challenge. 'All we'll need is a tank of invisible leeches, a household sponge, and some babyccino cups from the coffee shop.'

'What?' Jess glared at me. 'No!'

'Do you have a better idea?'

'Remember Mrs Spires said she has a check-up with the doctor on Friday morning?'

'Oh yeah,' I said. 'It must be Dr Salmon.'

'Why must it be Dr Salmon?' Miss Fortress said.

'Because everyone around here sees Dr Salmon,' Jess said.

'He's about one hundred years old and has known me since I was born.' I looked at Miss Fortress. 'Don't you see Dr Salmon?'

'I can't risk registering with a GP,' Miss Fortress said. 'Too many questions about who I am and where I've come from.'

'So what do you do when you're ill?' Jess asked.

'Stay at home. Eat soup. Contemplate the hopelessness of life.'

Me and Jess looked at her and I felt sorry for her again.

'Have you heard anything exciting on the police radio?' I said.

'There's a bit of chat about Sean Darryl Lamb,

the convict I told you about last time,' she said. 'And the chemistry between Jack and Rose is definitely hotting up – it's fascinating to listen to.'

'If we could plant Bob in Dr Salmon's office,' I said, 'he might be able to get a look at Mrs Spires' files.'

'Dr Salmon will bring them up on the computer when she's there for her appointment,' Jess said.

'That's actually a good idea,' I said. 'Great job, agent.'

'Don't patronise me.'

'Sounds like you two have something to be getting on with now,' Miss Fortress said, standing up and pushing us towards the classroom door. 'Let me know what you find out.'

She shut the door behind us.

'It'll be easy to find a hiding place for Bob,' Jess said. 'Dr Salmon has had that office for about twenty years, and I don't think he's ever cleaned it. But how will we get Bob in there in the first place?'

'Leave that to me, Jessticles. I have an amazing plan.'

'Mum, I need to see Dr Salmon,' I said when I got home from school.

Mum was busy in the cupboard under the stairs, so all I could see was her bottom and the back of her legs. 'Is this like the time you thought you had a robot insect living under your skin?' Her voice came out from the depths of the cupboard.

'No.'

'Or the time you thought the government had planted a computer chip in your brain to turn you into a human weapon?'

'No,' I said. 'What are you doing in there?'

'Trying to take a metre reading for the electricity. There's a shortage or something and they're talking about putting us all on rations. Rations! At Christmas!'

'But more importantly, Mum,' I said. 'Can you make me an appointment asap?'

'Or is this like the time you thought you had leprosy because you accidentally brushed your sleeve on someone's scabby elbow?'

'No, Mum – this is serious!'

'I don't want to disbelieve you, darling, but you said that all those other times, too.'

'This is legit!' I said. 'I have tummy troubles.

I've had them for a while but I didn't want to worry you.' My ear farted and the stink leaked through the air like a Ribena spill on a school shirt.

Mum finally backed up out of the cupboard. 'You should have said something before. It's nothing to be embarrassed about.'

'I'm at a sensitive age, Mum,' I said, picking at my fingernails.

'I'll call and make one,' she said. 'We'll go together.'

This was the trickiest part of the plan. 'I can go by myself, Mum.'

'I'd rather go with you this time, Alex. If you're serious about needing to see a doctor, then I should be with you.'

'Ugh. I'm almost a teenager, you know,' I said, knowing there was no point in arguing and I stomped up the stairs to text Jess: 'Getting apt for Doc Sal on Thurs after school. U nd to make 1 4 Fri pm to collect B.'

Instead of a text back, I got a WhatsApp notification: 'Jess added you to the group *Plans.*' Group members: Jess, Dave and Alex.

I opened WhatsApp. Jess was typing. 'No way

I'm making fake doc appointment. D has idea for collecting B.'

First things first: 'Alex changed name of group to *Secret Plans for Amazing Agents (and also Jessticles).*'

Trust Jess to not be able to handle telling a few little lies to help our mission. 'Fine – *chicken emoji, geek emoji.* D best man 4 job anyway, *100 emoji.*'

Dave typing. 'I'm due appt for psoriasis and mum working at hosp on Fri, so can go without her. Will grab Bob when there but will need distraction for Dr S??? *thinking emoji.*'

Jess started typing, so I typed really fast to get my reply in first. The small victories can be the most pleasing. 'Leave distract 2 me. TY Dave, U R backbone of the team, *perfect sign emoji.*' Then I added, 'D = backbone. B *fish emoji* = brain. A = *heart emoji.*'

Dave typing. Jess typing. 'Don't even ask him, D.'

Dave typing. 'Sorry, J – have to, *tongue poking, squinty eyes emoji.* What body part is J???'

I thought for a second. She might not be able to tell a lie, but she was still the bravest person I knew. 'J is the ba…' I started typing but was interrupted by a notification. 'Jess left the conversation.'

10

Da'Mishon

Before we could get on with planting Bob at the doctor to spy on Mrs Spires' appointment, we had another Zumba class to look forward to. Jess and I planned to keep an eye on the behaviour of the ladies in the group (and Alan too, just in case) and try to find some evidence against Da'Shon, all while we were working on the routine for the flash Zumba Christmas special, world-record-breaking attempt. Our main aim was to get a look in his bag, in case there were any of those mystery pots in there.

Mum and Nanny were really happy when Jess and I wanted to go back to Zumba. Well, Mum went all smiley and had tears in her eyes and Nanny gave me and Jess five pounds each, so that was a result.

When we got to the leisure centre, Angel was on the reception desk, as always, looking bored, as always. But she glanced up as we walked in.

'Four for Zumba, please,' Mum said, handing over a twenty-pound note. 'And are the fitness bands still full price?' She pointed at a stack of shiny boxes behind the desk. They were the fitness bands that everyone in Zumba had, and they looked sick, like Apple-quality sick.

'Discounts only for over-sixties,' Angel said. 'Are you over sixty?'

Nanny laughed and Mum looked embarrassed. 'Not quite yet,' she said. 'Maybe I'll put one on my Christmas list.'

'I'll get you one, Mum,' I said, feeling a bit sorry for her because Angel thought she looked as old as Nanny. 'How much?'

'Three hundred,' Angel said.

'Seriously?' I said. 'Pounds?'

'Thanks for the thought, darling, but they're a bit much at full price.' Mum ruffled my hair.

'Only thirty pounds for me,' Nanny said, flashing hers about.

'What does it do?' asked Jess.

'It counts steps, checks my heart-rate and tells me how many calories I should be eating,' Nanny said. 'It also reminds me when to get my medications and it can tell me if I'm starting to come down with something, so I can take preventative measures.'

'Like stocking up on nice food and firing up the Xbox?' I said.

'Like taking extra vitamins and getting plenty of rest,' Nanny laughed. 'And it can give me a printout of my stats so I can keep track.'

'How does it do that?' Jess said. 'Do you connect it to your computer?'

'Exactly, dear,' Nanny said. 'It's ridiculously easy. Even I can do it!'

'I hope you're being safe online, Nanny,' I said. 'The cyber world is dangerous if you don't know what you're doing.'

'I wonder if your data is protected?' Mum said.

'It's one hundred per cent safe,' Angel said without looking up from her phone. 'The only person with access to your data is you.'

My ear rumbled and a smell like last week's bins spread across the reception.

'We should get a move on,' Mum said, obviously embarrassed because of my stink. 'Good thing we have that appointment on Thursday, Alex.'

I nodded and went through the barrier, but I had multiple agenty thoughts whirling around my head.

'Why would Angel lie about the data being secure?' Jess whispered.

'It could just be that it's her job to sell them,' I said. 'It's not like she's doing anything else while she's sitting there.'

'But who do you think the data is shared with?' Jess said. 'Who would even want that information?'

'I don't know who else would be interested, but it would really help us out if we could get our hands on it.' I put my index fingers on each side of my forehead and made a whirring noise.

'What the hell are you doing?' Jess hissed.

'Storing the information for later,' I said. 'Now, let's focus on Da'Shon. I hope you brought some appropriate footwear this time. I heard Eileen saying you stunk out her trainers at the weekend.'

'The only thing stinking around here is you,' Jess said.

All the usual people were at the class and, as we warmed up to Nicki Minaj (one of the songs with swears in it, like we were a bunch of bad-As), I took the time to look around at everyone. They all seemed in good shape for people their age, easily keeping up with the music and loving every second. If anything, Eileen looked ten years younger than she had before her collapse.

'Right then, you sexy things,' Da'Shon said, in a way that made everyone laugh. 'Back to our Zumba flash-mob, Christmas special, world-record-breaking routine. Let's see who can remember what we learnt last class. From the top.'

As the song started playing, my mind went blank. I did the first couple of steps and shoulder rolls, and then I got stuck. I looked over at Jess for some help but she was flipping worse than me – stood there like a Bambi deer who's just seen a hunter pointing a shotgun at her.

But the rest of the class were on it. They shoulder-shimmied and criss-crossed. They body-rolled and booty-shook. I tried to keep my agent head on and not actually look at the movements because I didn't want to have nightmares for the rest of my life, but I can tell you that they were all on point. And they didn't just do the moves; they *did* the moves.

We were being out-danced by a room of old ladies (and Alan), including some who had literally just been dead. I didn't want to think I'd underestimated them, but perhaps I'd underestimated them. It wouldn't happen again.

I'm ashamed to say it, but I pretty much forgot the mission and focused on my dancing instead. I soon had the biggest sweat on ever, but it felt kind of good. Before I knew it, the music stopped and Da'Shon said, 'Good work, people, we are going to crush everyone else in that flash mob. Not that it's a competition.' He winked. 'Let's finish with some stretches and then I want you all practising the moves for next time, especially you two in the back.' He took a swig of water and looked right at Jess.

I let out a little snort of laughter. I couldn't tell if Jess went red because she was already the colour of Superman's eye lasers.

I watched Da'Shon as he took us through the stretches. It was hard to believe he was a bad guy. Sure, he worked us hard and he was super-strict.

And he was lying about things. And he was putting weird substances in the food of people who were collapsing and dying. But I liked him. Maybe this was how Jess felt about Taran, though, and she was the wrongest she could ever be about him. I sighed. Being a world-class agent was hard.

When everyone left the studio, me and Jess hung back.

'Distract him,' I whispered. 'I'm going to look through his bag.' And then, before she could argue as I knew she would, I called out, 'Da'Shon, Jess has something she wants to ask you.'

Da'Shon turned and came over. 'Just changing my shoes,' I said, walking to the end of the room where I'd cunningly left my bag next to Da'Shon's. He had his back to me; Jess just had to keep him busy.

'Yes, Jess, what can I do for you?' I heard Da'Shon say.

'Err…' she hesitated. 'I wanted to ask you for some Zumba tips.'

Yesss! I high-fived her in my head. Excellent distraction question.

I knelt down in front of the bags and unzipped Da'Shon's.

'First of all,' Da'Shon said to Jess, 'the fact that you're here and you're trying means you're a warrior, and you shouldn't feel ashamed if it doesn't come easy.'

He was so nice. I rummaged through the contents of his bag.

'Your main trouble is not that you can't learn the moves or that you don't have rhythm,' Da'Shon said. 'It's that you're afraid to let go.'

'Amen to that!' I almost shouted, but I didn't. Instead I opened a notebook at the bottom of the bag and started reading what was inside.

'Zumba is about joy,' Da'Shon carried on. 'You can't take yourself seriously and you've gotta stop worrying about what you look like.'

'I find that … hard sometimes,' Jess said. And I knew it was tough for her to admit that, so I was super proud.

Inside the notebook was a shopping list written on a torn-off strip of envelope. It didn't have a list of poisons on it, but when I went to put it back, I noticed something in one of the ragged corners. There were a couple of wavy black lines stamped on it that looked familiar. The rest of the image had been ripped off, but it really looked like the tentacles of an octopus. I stuffed it in my pocket.

'Lots of people do. But it just doesn't matter. You think when Alan first came here he wasn't embarrassed? Surrounded by beautiful ladies who were more experienced than him?'

'I guess he was,' Jess said.

I couldn't find anything else useful in Da'Shon's bag, so I carefully zipped it back up.

'He was a nervous wreck and I know he won't mind me telling you that,' Da'Shon laughed. 'But he stopped worrying, loosened up, and look at him now.'

'Alan's got some sick moves,' I said, walking over to them.

'He sure has,' said Da'Shon. 'And you will have too.' He looked down at my feet. 'You didn't change your shoes.'

'I remembered I like the squelchy noise sweaty feet make in trainers,' I said. 'We'd better catch up with Mum and Nanny. Thanks, Da'Shon.'

'See you next class.' He waved and walked over to his stuff.

'Did you find anything?' Jess said, when we were safely out of the room.

'This!' I said, showing her the piece of envelope. 'I know it's not the whole picture, but what does this look like to you?'

Jess frowned. 'It looks a bit like Angel's octopus tattoo.'

'That's exactly what I thought, Jessticles. We need to work out what this means.'

Two awesome things had come out of Da'Mishon. One was the octopus clue and the other, though I obvs didn't say it out loud, was that it had been kind of good for Jess.

11

Discussing Poo

When me and Mum arrived at the health centre, I found it hard to be chill. I was really excited about planting Bob in Dr Salmon's office – it was going to be super-tricky and dangerous, and as you know my middle name is Danger. Not Sidney like my mum says it is.

We waited to see the reception lady. Mum doesn't like using the auto-check-in because she doesn't trust it, and I don't like using it cos it's a touchscreen and who wants to put their hands on something that has been touched by a million sick people?

It was only a minute until the appointment, and the reception lady didn't look up from her computer where she was tapping away. I could feel Mum getting stressed because she hates being late. She looked at her watch a bunch of times, even though there was a clock right in front of her and she knew what the time was. I don't know why she didn't just go up to the lady and tell her we were waiting. Grown-ups are so weird sometimes. Then she did a small cough but the lady still didn't look up.

I couldn't stand it anymore. 'Hey, reception lady,' I said. 'I'm here for my appointment.'

The lady finally looked up, obviously annoyed but trying to look surprised.

'Oh, I didn't see you there,' she said, which was a big fat lie and my ear made a toxic pong. 'I'll be with you in a moment.'

She stood up and walked slowly over to a printer, taking a sheet of paper from it and bringing it back to her desk. She put it down and got back into her chair, spending ages adjusting her seat. I rolled my eyes in the manner of Jess, and noticed the name at the top of the printout. It was Sean Darryl Lamb – the guy Miss Fortress had been talking about – and it looked like a copy of his medical records. The reception lady slid it into a brown file that was sitting under her coffee mug. As she opened it, I swear I saw a small black octopus stamped on the inside.

'A dossier,' I whispered.

'What name is it?' she snapped at me.

'Alex Danger Sparrow for Doctor Salmon,' I said.

The lady seemed surprised and just stared at me.

'We'll take a seat,' I said.

We sat in the waiting area, with the reception lady staring at us the whole time. It was a big room with loads of rows of uncomfortable seats and ferny plants in the corners. The walls were covered with posters about random diseases and what to do if you discover a weird rash on your body. By the time we'd waited twenty minutes, I was certain I had scarlet fever, hyperemesis and Ebola. I rolled up my trouser legs to look for inflamed veins.

'Does my right leg look fatter than my left to

you?' I said to Mum. 'And what's a long-haul flight?'

'Alex, you don't have deep vein thrombosis,' Mum said. I was just about to ask her how she could be sure, when the speaker said, "Alll-ex Spar-row to surg-erry three, Doc-toooor Sallll-mon.'

I jumped up and ran through the sliding doors to Dr Salmon's office, knocking on the door with my most 'I'm honestly, totally, believably sick' knock. I'd done it many times before.

'Come in!' came a voice from inside.

I opened the door, trying to keep my bag steady so that Bob wouldn't have a go at me for swishing him around. He hates that.

'Ah, young Mr Sparrow, and Mrs Sparrow.' Dr Salmon smiled. 'What can I do for you today?'

I sat in the chair closest to his desk and casually looked around for potential hiding places while I spoke to him. 'I've got stomach troubles, Dr Salmon,' I said. 'Bad ones.'

'It's been going on for a few months,' Mum said. 'Nothing to stop him from going about his normal business, but there's definitely an issue.'

'I see,' Dr Salmon said. 'What are the symptoms?'

'He has the most terrible, foul smelling...' Mum went a bit pink in the cheeks and half mouthed the next word, '...wind.'

'Is there any pain with the wind?' Dr Salmon asked.

I was going to say no, but I thought it might be an opportunity to get a bit of sympathy from Mum, which couldn't be a bad thing right before Christmas. 'It does hurt a bit,' I said, making a sad face, which conveniently made a disgusting smell come out of my ear. 'Like now.'

'And is it constant, or only at certain times, like when you've eaten?' Dr Salmon said.

'It's on and off but doesn't seem to be connected to food.' If Mum put me on some awful diet it would be the worst thing in the world. 'It just sometimes happens.'

'What about the toilet? Any blood or diarrhoea?'

'Not that I've noticed,' Mum said.

'What the fudge, Mum, have you been looking at my poos?' I said.

'It's my job as your mother to check your poo,' Mum said.

'What about my human rights?' I stood up. 'To poo privately and without fear of inspection.'

'I'm sorry, darling,' Mum said. 'But I was worried.'

'I'd like you to keep a diary,' Dr Salmon said. 'Of your diet and the times when you get the pain and the wind.'

'I don't know,' I said, 'that sounds kind of boring.'

'Of course we'll do it,' Mum said.

'And if you can collect a stool sample and bring it in at your earliest convenience, we'll run some tests,' Dr Salmon said.

'I don't see how that will help, but I'll try to get one if you think it's important and Mum promises not to get mad at me.'

'Dr Salmon isn't talking about the kind of stool you sit on, darling,' Mum said.

'Huh?'

'A stool is what we call a lump of your number twos.'

'Wait,' I said. 'You want me to bring you a piece of my poo?'

'You'd be surprised how much we can learn from a stool sample,' Dr Salmon laughed. Actually, no, he didn't laugh – he chuckled. He was definitely a chuckler. 'I'll give you a tinkle when the results come back.'

'Thank you, Dr Salmon.' Mum stood up.

'There's something else I want to discuss with Dr Salmon,' I said. 'In private.'

'What is it?' Mum said. 'Surely you can talk about it with me here.'

'No, it has to be man-to-man. It's to do with puberty.'

'Can't you talk to your dad about it instead?' Mum looked embarrassed.

'Unless I'm very much mistaken, Dad is not a medical professional. And I think I've had my privacy disrespected enough for one day.'

Mum looked at me. 'Fine. I'll wait outside.'

'So,' the doctor said when Mum had left. 'What can I help you with, young sir?'

'I have some questions, mostly about how I can make my voice go lower and grow extra hair on parts of my body but not others.'

'Puberty isn't something you can force, Alex, it happens when it's good and ready. It can be an awkward time, but it's natural and it will pass.'

'Do you have any leaflets that I can take home and read?' I asked.

'Yes, there should be some in the waiting room,' Dr Salmon said.

'Could you please get them for me? I want to make sure I get the right ones and I'll be too embarrassed to pick them up myself. And then could you give them to my mum to put in her bag so I don't have to carry them? I'll wait here. Thanks!'

Dr Salmon gave me a funny look and took in a little sniff of the stink my lies had sent hurtling out into his office. It gave him the motivation he needed not to try to argue with me and to go and pick up the leaflets.

As soon as he was out of the room, I pulled Bob out of my bag and put him carefully on a shelf behind some dusty books and a statue of a man playing golf but where he should still get a good view of the computer screen on the desk. 'Good luck, Bob,' I whispered. 'Dave will be in tomorrow to collect you.' I double-checked he couldn't be seen easily from Dr Salmon's seat, and then I sat back down in mine. Just in time.

Dr Salmon came back into the room. 'Right, I've given your mother the information you requested, and if you can get me that sample, we'll take things from there.'

'Thanks, Dr Salmon.' I stood up and headed for

the door. I always hated leaving Bob on his spying missions, worried that someone would find him and he'd be flushed down a toilet or thrown in an aquarium. I glanced up at his spot on the shelf. 'I'll see you soon.'

After my appointment, I got Mum to drop me at Dave's house, which wasn't hard because she loves Dave more than she loves me. Jess was already there.

'How did it go?' she said.

'Agent Bob is in place. He's behind the golf-man statue, FYI.'

'I hope he'll be OK,' Jess said.

'He actually seemed more excited than usual,' I said. 'You know how interested he is in medical science stuff.'

Dave sat down in his spinny computer chair. 'Hopefully one day I'll be good enough to hack high-security organisations. Then you won't have to send Bob into as many places.'

'Is Dr Salmon high security?' I said.

'Yeah, anything medical is,' Dave nodded. 'Encryption for days.'

'We should see what we can find out about Sean Darryl Lamb,' I said.

'On it,' Dave said, tapping and clicking away while me and Jess watched.

'That's all of them,' Dave said after an hour of trawling through Insta, Twitter and a bunch of other sites. 'He has no social-media accounts and I can't find a single image of him online.'

'What sort of person doesn't have any social-media accounts?' I pulled my hat off and rubbed my eyes with it.

'The sort of person who doesn't want to be found,' said Jess.

'OK. News next,' Dave said.

'In the movie, they'll have to make this part into a montage,' I said. 'No offence, Dave.'

'You mean people wouldn't want to watch hours of me sitting at my computer?' Dave laughed. 'Surprising.'

Me and Jess sort of drifted off after a bit. I got off the beanbag and lay down on Dave's bed, tired after a week of undercover ops. And Zumba. I might have fallen asleep, just for a minute.

'Hey, guys,' Dave said. 'You're going to want to see this.'

I rolled off the bed and flew over to Dave.

On his computer screen was an article from a Cherry Tree Lane news website. The headline was 'Man Found Guilty of Attempted Burglary'.

'Sean Darryl Lamb of Bourne Avenue, Topgate, has been sentenced to four years in prison,' I read. 'It says he tried to rob an old lady's house in Cherry Tree Lane.'

'But why is a receptionist at the doctor's making a file about him? And how are he, Da'Shon and Angel connected to the black octopus?' Jess sighed.

'We need to keep our eyes open: look out for that octopus everywhere we go. There must be some way of finding out what it is.'

'I'll keep looking online,' Dave said. 'I'll let you know if I find anything.'

'The Mystery of the Black Octopus,' I said. 'We are literally living the dream.'

12

Bob Drops One

We didn't find out anything more that night – Mum picked us up a few minutes later. She dropped Jess home and for once I was thankful, rather than annoyed, that she insisted on waiting until she'd seen Jess's mum open the door and wave at us before she drove off. Between convicted criminals and the sinister Black Octopus gang apparently infiltrating our town, there was danger all around us. We were going to have to be more careful.

I slept really badly that night, even though I

was super-exhausted. I got up a few times to peep out of the window, and I thought a lot about Bob all alone at the health centre. Mr Prickles climbed up on my bed and kept me company, keeping watch when I finally dozed off.

The next day at school dragged. At afternoon break, I took the plastic pot Dr Salmon had given me and settled myself in the toilets for my usual 2pm poo. Once my sample was ready, I wrapped the pot up in a brown paper bag. Now it was all a matter of timing. Dave's appointment was at 3.35pm, but you pretty much never got in until about fifteen or twenty minutes after your time. Dave had a text loaded and ready to send as soon as he was called to surgery three by the robot voice.

At 3.42pm, I was outside the surgery in the car with Mum and Lauren, stalling.

'Would you like me to take it in for you, darling?' Mum said.

'No, Mum, I'm almost a man. I can do it myself.'

'It's just we've been sitting here for almost ten minutes.' Mum reached out for my poo bag. 'Let me take it.'

'I'm bored, Mummy,' Lauren whinged in the back from her booster seat.

'Shut up, Lauren,' I said. 'I'm psyching myself up.'

'Why does Alex have to give his poo to the doctor anyway?' Lauren said. 'Is it because he always makes bad smells?'

'SHUT UP, LAUREN!' I turned and glared at her.

'Come on, you two, that's enough.' Mum looked at her watch. 'Alex, we really need to get back.'

'You people are supposed to be my family,' I said. 'I don't ask for much from you in life and I try to be the best son and brother that I can. Do you need me to remind you about all of the many millions of times that I've gone out of my way for you?'

'Yes,' Lauren said.

I ignored her. 'If I need a few minutes to summon my courage to undertake a personal quest of the gravest nature, the least you can do...' I felt my phone vibrate in my pocket. 'Never mind, I'm going in. Back in a sec.'

I leapt out of the car and up the steps to the surgery, strutting through the automatic doors like I wasn't there to deliver a piece of my own poo.

The mean lady was at the reception desk, telling someone on the phone that they had absolutely no appointments for at least a week. My ear buzzed, of course. I shook my head at her as I walked past.

I bowled across the waiting room, through the sliding door and down the corridor to surgery three. I knocked on the door.

'I'm with a patient,' Dr Salmon's voice called out.

'I'm sorry, but this is urgent,' I said, knocking again. I heard Dr Salmon's chair creak as he got up, and a few seconds later the door opened.

'Mr Sparrow?' He looked surprised. Dave gave me a thumbs-up from the chair next to Dr Salmon's desk.

'I have it,' I said.

'Have what?'

'The item you requested as soon as possible.'

'Come again?'

'Hold on a sec,' I said, reaching to close Dr Salmon's door behind him. 'Sorry, random young man, this is a private matter,' I said to Dave who was trying not to laugh. 'I brought the poo,' I said to Dr Salmon.

'Good, good. You can leave it with Susan on reception.' He turned to go back into his office.

'I'm not leaving it with her,' I said. 'She pretends she can't see people when they're standing there waiting, and I know she can. She can't be trusted with something so important.' Or actually anything at all, because she's clearly part of the Black Octopus gang.

Dr Salmon looked like he was trying not to laugh. 'Very well, I'll take it. We wouldn't want it falling into the wrong hands.'

I gave him the bag. 'You won't believe how tricky it was to get this. I tried to catch some as it was falling into the toilet, but I missed. So I had to put my hand into the water to scoop some out, but all the pieces were too big and I had to try to break some off.'

'That does sound like a bit of an ordeal,' Dr Salmon said. 'Well done for getting it to me, and I'll be in touch with the results. Now, I must get back to my patient.'

He opened his office door. Surely that was enough time? I walked back out to the car.

'Can we go, Mum? It's getting late and I really need to get back.'

She gave me a look.

My phone vibrated in my pocket. It was a text from Dave with the fish emoji and a thumbs-up emoji.

'By the way,' I said. 'Dave and Jess are coming over in a bit.'

Mum always loved it when Dave came over for dinner, and she chatted to him for ever, so we had to wait ages to get some time on our own.

'Here he is,' Dave said, pulling Bob's jar out of his bag. 'He seems fine.'

We tipped Bob gently back into his tank and gave him some time to say 'hi' to Elle, and to eat and swim a couple of circuits to stretch out his fins. I always hated this part – waiting for the debrief. A debrief is what you do after an important mission when you update each other on what's happened. It has nothing to do with losing your pants.

'So, did you see Mrs Spires?' I said. 'Is her blood full of poison and zombie bacteria?'

Jess twitched. 'Mrs Spires is extremely healthy for a sixty-six-year-old female human.'

'Son of a biscuit, that's so annoying.' I thumped

the breakfast bar with my fist. It hurt but I styled it out.

'Bob saw the results of her blood test and they were textbook healthy. So it seems like Da'Shon can't be poisoning the Zumba class.'

'Did he find out what caused her death at least?'

'The doctor remains unsure, which Bob found to be most disconcerting considering he's supposed to be an experienced medical professional.'

'Another flipping dead end!' I huffed.

'How can someone die for days, then come back to life in their coffin, for no apparent reason?' Dave said. 'And Dr Salmon knows everything, so if he can't figure it out, how will we?'

'Dr Salmon has been a doctor for a million years. And he knows everyone in Cherry Tree Lane. You're right, if he can't make sense of what happened to Mrs Spires, it's got to be something totally new or crazy.' Jess leant forward on the breakfast bar and propped her chin in her hands.

'Like something caused by a maniac-genius scientist.' I jumped up. 'It's got to be Montgomery McMonaghan. He's doing something to the Zumba ladies. I might not know what, and I might not know how, but I know he's behind it.'

'Even supposing that's true, how is Da'Shon connected? And this Sean Darryl Lamb?' Dave said.

'Any why target a group of old ladies?' Jess said.

'I don't know,' I sighed. 'But we're going to get a breakthrough soon – it always happens in the movies when things seem hopeless.'

'Hold on a sec,' Jess said. 'Bob is saying something.'

She jiggled about on her stool for a moment. And when I say stool, I mean the kind you sit on in the kitchen, not the brown kind that you take to your doctor in a plastic pot.

'He wants to see the picture from the Cricket Club again.'

Jess scrolled through her pics and held the photo up so Bob could get a good look, then looked up at me with wide eyes. 'Bob says it's definitely him.'

'Definitely who?' Me and Dave said at the same time.

'The man in the photo that you thought was *our* Montgomery McMonaghan who had somehow transported himself back in time, he isn't our Montgomery McMonaghan at all.'

'He isn't?' This was confusing.

'The boy next to him is our Montgomery McMonaghan – looks just like him – I don't know how we didn't notice.'

We peered at the photo.

'Yeah, he has the devilish good looks and a crazy glint in his eyes,' I said. 'So why does the old guy look so much like him?'

'Because the old guy is Montgomery McMonaghan senior. He's Montgomery McMonaghan's dad!'

'And Bob worked this out how?'

'He worked it out when Montgomery McMonaghan senior walked in for an appointment with Dr Salmon.'

'Shut. Up.' I looked at Bob. 'Any other bombs you want to drop?'

'Just one more big one,' Jess said. 'Montgomery McMonaghan senior lives in Cherry Tree Lane. And Bob has his address.'

'So I guess you're pretty pleased with yourself?' I looked at Bob. 'Dropping the breakthrough moment like a boss.'

Bob just carried on swimming around his tank, but I swear he looked like the smuggest goldfish ever.

13

McMonadad

The chance to find out more about Montgomery McMonaghan was too good to pass up. It was the weekend, and all we could think about was going to the older Montgomery McMonaghan's house to see if we could find anything that would lead us to our nemesis, or connect him to the Zumba mystery. It was too much of a coincidence that a zombie outbreak was starting in the town where a McMonaghan lived. I had to find out more.

On Saturday morning, Jess and me went to the

animal sanctuary for our shift. It was always nice to check in on our friends who had all been part of our last adventure, like Sir Blimmo the tortoise and Raymond rat, who were well and happy. We told Harry the horse about Zumba class and showed him some of the routines, because he loves to dance, then left him practising the moves in his stable. The angry deer had made a full recovery from being knocked down and been released back into the wild. After Boris and Noodle the guinea pigs had turned out to be double agents, they'd gone into hiding, so the school needed some replacement animals to look after, and Piper the rabbit had moved to Cherry Tree Lane school with another rabbit called Wiggles. Rex and Mrs Fernandes, who ran the sanctuary, had never found the corn snake, but I liked to think he was living a happy life somewhere.

Once we'd said 'hi' to everyone, we went back to discussing ways to get into MM's house, without making him call the police, or even worse, his son.

'Carol singing,' I said.

'People don't let carol singers into their house,' said Jess. 'And with your singing voice, he probably wouldn't even open the door.'

'We could disguise ourselves as plumbers?'

'He's not going to believe we're plumbers. And, even if he did, I for one wouldn't let you anywhere near my pipes.'

'Wouldn't want to go near your pipes anyway,' I said. 'And do you want to suggest something, instead of just being annoying about all my ideas?'

'I'm trying to be realistic! Whether Montgomery McMonaghan is behind the Zumba weirdness or not, there's a lot at stake!' Her voice went all loud and annoyed.

'It's my mum and nanny in danger, don't you think I know there's a lot at stake? And of course he's behind it. We just need to find proof!' I shouted back.

We raked poo in silence for a few minutes.

'Sorry I shouted,' I said.

'I'm sorry, too,' Jess said.

'Buddies?' I said, holding out my rake.

'Buddies.' She clinked rakes with me, which everyone knows is the greatest proof of buddyism there is. Not to be confused with Buddhism, which, as I understand it, is quite different and has nothing to do with rakes.

'We need to make him like and trust us so he'll talk,' said Jess.

'Lucky for us it's Christmas, and people are a lot more trusting at this time of year.'

'Maybe we could use that, somehow. What do you think he's like?'

'Well…' I scattered some fresh straw on the ground in the enclosure. 'All we know, from what Miss Fortress said, is that he has a difficult relationship with his son and doesn't see him very often.'

'And his wife died a few years ago.'

'So he's probably quite sad,' I said. 'And lonely.'

'Maybe he'll be happy to have some company, even if it's us,' Jess said.

'OK, so Christmas is the time of giving, right? We could do that thing we had to do in year one for Harvest Festival.'

'When we put together baskets of rubbish food and gave it to the old people in the area.' Jess stopped scattering and stood up. 'That could work.'

'We'll go in our school uniforms with a few packets of biscuits. He'll let us in and tell us everything we need to know about his son. We'll only tie him up if we absolutely have to.'

'We are not tying him up.'

'I said tying him up because I thought you'd prefer that to tasering,' I said.

'Why does it always come back to tasering with you?' Jess sighed. 'Do you think we'll be safe with him, though? We don't actually know him.'

'He's probably harmless, but let's take Dave too. Three of us and one of him. He won't stand a chance if it comes down to a Battle Royale. And we'll make sure my mum's nearby, just in case.' Not that I need my mum to back me up. Because I don't.

'That's the plan, then,' Jess said. 'When shall we do it?'

'This afternoon, of course. It's not long until Christmas, we have Zumba tomorrow, and we need to move things forward, fast. What's the point in waiting?'

'OK,' Jess nodded. Then she sniffed the air. 'I think it's going to snow.'

'Great, that can only work in our favour. Snow means old people get scared of being stuck in their houses, so he'll be extra glad of some packets of biscuits and a few tea bags. Anyway, how do you know it's going to snow?'

'I can always tell,' Jess shivered.

'OMG, you're Elsa.'

'I'm not Elsa.'

'But your hair! And your frosty nature, keeping people at a distance, even when you don't really want to! And you wear gloves LOADS.'

'I'm not Elsa. For goodness' sake, Alex.'

'Fine, fine.' I went inside to get some food for the rabbits and guinea pigs. When I got back to enclosure six, the wind was whipping around Jess, making some of her blonde hair come loose from her plait.

'Jess,' I side-eyed her. 'If it snows ... do you wanna build a snowman?'

'I hate you.'

Two hours later I was dressed in my school uniform and raiding the kitchen cupboards for stuff to take to old Montgomery's.

'What are you doing, Alex?' Mum said.

'Charity thing for school. We have to take a basket of food to an old person.'

'Why didn't you tell me before?' Mum put her hands on her hips.

'I forgot, I guess,' I said, and the loud ear fart

blocked out the sound of my mum sighing. 'Dave's coming,' I added, with a sneaky look.

'Oh well, I suppose it's a nice thing to do. And it is Christmas.'

'So you're good to give us a lift. Awesome.'

'You can't take that!' Mum looked at my pile of stuff on the counter – half a tub of gravy granules, a nearly full pack of chocolate Hobnobs, five tea bags and a satsuma.

'That's not very kind of you, Mum. It's Christmas and he's old.'

'Give me five minutes,' she said, pushing me out of the kitchen.

I got my coat and shoes, and when I went back into the kitchen Mum was tying a giant red bow on the handle of a basket filled with food. There was a fancy tin of biscuits, a jar of Dad's special coffee, some grapes and another fruit that was so posh I didn't even know what it was, a box of chocolates and a full, sealed pack of tea bags.

'Been keeping a secret stash of nice food, have we?' I raised an eyebrow at her.

'I always put a few bits away for Christmas,' she said. 'But I have time to replace these next week. Are we picking up Jess and Dave on the way?'

'Damn right we are.'

'Let's go then, and watch your language, please.'

Twenty minutes later, with Jess and Dave in the car, we pulled up at 77 Hazel Lane, aka the McMonaghan residence.

'How long do you think you'll be?' Mum said as we got out of the car.

'Difficult to say. You can listen to the radio while you wait, and here's a grape to tide you over.' I pulled a shrivelled one off the bunch in the basket.

'We need to get this right,' Jess said, as we walked up a tiny path to the front door. Montgomery McMonaghan's home was a narrow terraced house in the middle of a long row. His garden was small but tidy, with a lawn and some flower beds. There was a gnome dressed as a cricket person on one side of the door.

'It doesn't look like an evil lair,' I said as I stepped forward to ring his doorbell.

A much older version of the man in the cricket club photo opened the door. He looked a lot like Montgomery McMonaghan, with thick curly hair, but his was completely grey. His face was a bit wrinkled and he didn't have a beard like his son did. And although he had the same dark eyes, they didn't gleam with the same light of psychopathy.

'Hello,' he said. 'Can I help you?'

I decided I would need to take control of the situation and do all the talking, because, let's face it, Jess was rubbish at this stuff. 'Hi, Mr McMonaghan, we're from Cherry Tree Lane Primary School.'

'Are you collecting money for something?' He started patting his pockets. 'I'm sure I have some change I can give you.'

I felt Jess relax beside me. This guy couldn't be a super-villain like his son.

I had to focus really hard on controlling my ear as I launched into my pitch – I didn't want to make a stink that would stop him from inviting us into his house.

'We're not here to collect money from you. We're here to give you something.'

Jess smiled and held out the food basket.

'For me?' He looked surprised.

'We're doing a Christmas thing at school where we give food baskets out to people in the neighbourhood. And we got you.' I gave him a dazzling smile.

'That's very kind,' he said. 'I don't remember signing up to anything like that, though.'

'People were nominated,' I said, thinking fast. 'Maybe someone from the cricket club put your name forward?'

'That could be it.' His face brightened up. 'I don't know what to say.'

He had actual tears in his eyes.

I looked at Dave and Jess and I knew they were thinking what I was thinking – that we couldn't just get information from him.

I started coughing (I'd practised in the bathroom before we left) and kept going, hacking away like I was about to drop dead.

'Would you like a glass of water, son?' MM senior said.

I nodded through my desperate coughs, leaning forward as Dave rubbed me on my back.

'You'd better come in.' Montgomery senior stepped back and we walked into his hallway. He closed the door behind us. 'Take a seat in there,' he said, pointing at an open door on the right. 'I'll get that water.'

We walked into the lounge, which was small but cosy, and being kept toasty warm by an old-fashioned heater in the chimney wall. There was a two-seater sofa and an armchair that didn't match but which was obviously his favourite place to sit because it was really worn out and had a bottom-shaped dent in the seat. We all squished on to the sofa. In front of us was probably the smallest TV I've ever seen. The screen wasn't much bigger than a sheet of A4 paper, but what it lacked in screen size it made up for in blockiness. It was like a cube. And I couldn't see a Sky box so I'm pretty sure he only had a couple of channels.

'I didn't realise people lived this way,' I whispered.

I managed to tear my eyes away from his prehistoric TV long enough to notice all the framed photographs he had on the shelves. There were lots of a blonde lady, who must have been his wife, and lots of his son, from baby pictures, through primary and secondary school shots, and then they just stopped. There were none of Montgomery junior as an adult.

Mr McMonaghan came into the room with a glass of water. 'Get this down you, son,' he said, handing me the glass.

I gulped the water, even though it was obviously

tap, not bottled, and stopped coughing. 'Thank you, sir,' I said. 'You probably saved my life.'

He laughed and picked up the food basket from the table where Jess had left it. 'This is, well, let's just say you've made an old man very happy. I'm chuffed to bits. Shall we open these biscuits now, and have one?' He peeled the seal from the tin and offered them round to all of us. Me and Dave both took one, but Jess said, 'I can't, thank you, I'm vegan.'

'Oh.' He crinkled his forehead. 'Some grapes, then?'

He put grapes on a plate for Jess, got us all glasses of juice and made himself a cup of tea, then he sat down in his chair and offered us another biscuit.

He really was properly nice and I felt a bit guilty that we'd stolen his address from his medical records and lied to his face, just so we could find some stuff out. I didn't often feel guilty and I didn't like it at all.

'Is this your wife?' Jess said, pointing at one of the photos.

'Yes.' He smiled. 'That's my beautiful Maggie. She passed away a few years back and I miss her every day.'

'It looks like you were really happy together,' Dave said. 'Where was this one taken?'

Mr McMonaghan started to talk about his life with his wife and tell us the stories behind all their photos. I know that sounds really boring, but they actually did loads of interesting and funny stuff, and it was nice to listen to because it obviously made him so happy to remember. I was almost sorry to ask about MM junior.

'This must be your son,' I said, picking up a picture of Mr McMonaghan and his wife each holding the hand of a toddler-sized Montgomery junior.

'Yes, that's our Monty. He used to love it when we swung him as we walked along.'

'Is he grown up now?' Dave said.

'All grown up and doing his own thing. He's a bright boy and headstrong. He runs a successful business.' He said it in this way, like he was proud and sad at the same time. It was hard to keep asking questions about something that was obviously tough for him, but I reminded myself that we were there for a reason. Old Mr McMonaghan might be a properly nice bloke, but his son was dangerous. So I kept on.

'Will you be spending Christmas together?'

'Oh no, we haven't spent Christmas together for about twenty years. I haven't seen Monty at all since Maggie's funeral, and even then we hardly spoke.'

'Why is that?' I said. 'I can't imagine not seeing my dad for years.'

'It's complicated.' He sighed. 'We argued a lot. There were many things on which we didn't see eye to eye.'

'But you look so happy in the pictures,' said Jess. 'It seems a shame that you don't see each other now.'

Mr McMonaghan sipped his cup of tea. 'We're either too similar, or too different. I can never quite work out which.'

'Is there no way you could work things out?' Dave said. I think we'd all forgotten for a moment that this was super-villain Montgomery McMonaghan that we were talking about. We just wanted Mr McMonaghan to be happy.

'I don't think so.' He shook his head. 'I'd be happy to try to talk things through, but it's been so long and I'm certain he doesn't want anything to do with me. Although he does send me a

Christmas card every year.' His face brightened. 'It arrived today. I'll show you.'

He took a pile of papers from a shelf beside him and pulled out a big cream-coloured envelope. He passed it across to us with a small smile. Jess took it and slid the card out from inside. It had a drawing of a poshly decorated Christmas tree on the front, with fancy silver writing that said 'Season's Greetings'. Inside it just said, 'To Dad, Merry Christmas, Monty'.

'I think he must care about you still, or he wouldn't bother sending you a nice card,' I said.

'Do you think so?' Mr McMonaghan said.

'Definitely,' Jess said, reading the inside of the card again. I don't know what we were hoping to find in those few words of his handwriting, but she seemed as reluctant as I was to give it back.

Suddenly, Dave started having a coughing fit, almost as bad as mine.

'Let me get you some water.' Mr McMonaghan jumped up and left the room.

'Are you OK, Dave?' said Jess.

'Get the envelope,' he croaked between coughs. 'We need the envelope.'

Mr McMonaghan came back with the water.

I looked around the room while Dave was glugging it back. Fake coughing actually really hurts your throat, in case you didn't know. There were only two Christmas cards up on the shelf above the fire.

'I have just had the best idea,' I said. 'You should come to Zumba with us.'

'What's zoomer?' Mr McMonaghan said.

'Zumba,' I said. 'It's like fitness dancing, which sounds awful, I know, but it's actually really fun and there are lots of nice ladies there.'

'Are you trying to find me a lady-friend?' Mr McMonaghan said. For a moment I thought he was annoyed, but then he laughed. 'I'm not much of a dancer.'

'You should see Jess,' I said, and she kicked me hard in the leg.

'You should try it, Mr McMonaghan,' Dave said. 'It's only down the road, and if you hate it you don't have to go again.'

'We're doing a special Christmas thing at the moment,' said Jess. 'And we need as many people as possible to join in.'

'Is it all ladies, though?'

'No, we have an Alan,' I said. 'And he could use

a mate. It's a proper laugh, I promise. Please come.'

'I'll think about it,' he smiled. 'When's the next class?'

'It's…' Jess started.

'We're just waiting for confirmation,' I said. 'Give me your mobile number and I'll text you later.'

'I don't have a mobile.'

'What?' we all said at once.

He laughed again. 'No need for one.'

Honestly, it was the saddest thing I'd ever heard.

'Your email then?' I said.

'No email.'

'How do you communicate with the outside world?' I said.

'I have a home phone. I could give you that number.'

'Awesome. Do you mind if I write on this envelope? Thanks.' I got out a pen and scribbled 'Mr M' on the clean side without giving him a chance to say no. I took down his number and then we left, after making him promise that he would properly consider doing Zumba with us.

He waved us off looking a lot happier than he had when we arrived. It felt kind of nice that we cheered him up and, even though I'd only said it so we could get the envelope, which Dave wanted for some unknown reason, I really did hope he'd come to Zumba.

'How was it?' Mum said when we got in the car.

'Fine,' we all said at the same time. Everyone knows that 'fine' is the only acceptable answer to give when a grown-up asks about something you've been doing.

'Was he pleased with his basket?'

'He loved it,' Dave said. 'Thank you, Mrs Sparrow.'

And, of course, that was enough for my mum, who smiled at Dave in the mirror and hummed along with Christmas songs on the radio all the way home.

14

Biscuits

Dave had to go straight home for a family dinner, so we didn't get to ask him why he wanted the envelope. He ripped off the part with the phone number and gave it to me, then put the rest of the envelope in his pocket as he got out of the car.

'Why do you think he wanted that?' I asked Jess as soon as we were alone. 'I bet he has a cool forensics kit at home and he's going to dust it for prints.'

Jess snorted. 'Even if he did, how would that

help us? We already know that both Montgomery McMonaghans' prints will be on there.'

'He'll be putting it under one of those UV lights then,' I said, 'to see if there are any strange bodily fluids on it.'

'I'm pretty sure he won't.'

At that moment my mum walked into the kitchen. 'Jess, your mum just phoned. She's been called out on a late job and asked if you can stay here for tonight. I told her it's fine with me, if it's OK with you?'

'Yes, thanks, Mrs Sparrow, if you're sure you don't mind?'

'Of course not, we love having you here. Just give me five minutes and then we'll go and pick up some of your things.'

'Yesss!' I said. 'Sleepover!'

'Shall we do each other's make-up?' Jess said.

'Patchwork skin or zombies?'

'We did patchwork skin last time and you made me look like a pie chart. Let's go with zombies.'

'Ooh, with a Christmas twist?'

'Sure. Christmas zombies sounds good. I'll get my make-up kit.'

'And when you get back, we can WhatsApp Dave to see what he's planning with the envelope.'

'OK, see you in a bit.' Jess and Mum went out of the house, letting a gust of cold in as they opened the door. It still wasn't snowing but the outside world was quiet, like it was waiting for something to happen.

'Hey, Bob,' I said, leaning in front of his tank. 'I've been thinking about the family stuff, and there are some things you should see. There are lots of examples of families that are worth looking at – I'm going to put the Harry Potter audiobooks on for you, and I want you to pay special attention to the Weasleys. They're an awesome family. Then if you're interested in some more messed-up types, check out the Skywalkers and the Solos in the *Star Wars* franchise. You'll see what happens when there are ISSUES. And then...' I looked around to make sure nobody was listening '...you ought to know that families don't just have to be made up of your actual family. You can sort of adopt people, and they become part of your family. So you and Elle and Mr Prickles are part of my family. And Jess is, too.'

Bob eyeballed me.

'Yes, I know we're very different and we don't always get along, but that's part of it. If you watch

Guardians of the Galaxy volumes one and two, that might help you to understand.'

Bob and Elle looked at each other and flapped their fins a bit, like they were having a conversation. I turned away so it wouldn't look like I was listening in. They deserved their privacy.

Nanny Sparrow was over and Dad was home, so when Jess and Mum got back, we all ate dinner together.

'Could you get me some water, please, Alex?' Nanny said. 'The chicken is dry.'

Mum was busy cutting up Lauren's food and I could see her biting her lip. 'Maybe you're a little dehydrated from all your Zumba practice,' she said, looking at Nanny.

'About that,' I said. 'Me and Jess might have invited someone to join, is that OK?'

'Is it Dave?' Mum's face lit up. Honestly, I think she actually loved him more than me.

'No, Dave has band practice,' I said. 'It's actually the man we took the food basket to today.'

'What's this about a food basket?' said Nanny.

'Alex, Jess and Dave took a little hamper round to a Cherry Tree Lane resident today,' Mum said. 'Something they're doing for Christmas at school.'

'Is that where my nice coffee went?' Dad said.

'Calm down, I'll get you some more. It was for a good cause.' Mum stabbed a potato with her fork.

'I suppose,' Dad said. 'I'm guessing you gave him the tin of biscuits too?'

'They were really good biscuits,' I said, through a mouthful. 'I had, like, five.'

'I want a biscuit,' Lauren said. 'Why didn't I get a biscuit if Alex got a biscuit?'

'Because I was doing something kind,' I said, which made a bit of a stink come out.

'The biscuits weren't actually for Alex, but they were shared with him,' Mum said to Lauren. 'It's Christmas in a week – there will be plenty more biscuits for everyone.'

'I want to hear more about this biscuit man,' said Nanny.

'His name is Mr McMonaghan. His wife died a few years ago and he doesn't see his son,' Jess said.

'He doesn't have a mobile phone, his TV looked older than him, and he only had three Christmas cards. He needs our help.' I took a gulp of cordial. 'Also, he's really nice. He basically saved my life.'

'What?' Mum looked up. 'You didn't tell me this!'

'He means Mr McMonaghan gave him some water when he had a cough,' Jess said.

'It was a really bad cough.' I put my knife and fork on my plate. 'What's for dessert?'

'Finish your peas, please,' Mum said.

'So is Mr McMonaghan interested in Zumba?' Nanny asked.

'He's a bit shy,' said Jess. 'He might need persuading.'

'Which is where you come in, Nanny. If anyone can get him to Zumba, it's you. Will you phone him for us? Here's his number.'

I reached across the table to hand Nanny the torn off bit of envelope and 'accidentally' knocked the rest of my peas on to the floor. 'Oops, can't eat them now.'

'No dessert then,' Dad said.

'I remember another boy who never ate his peas,' said Nanny, looking at the telephone number, and then at Dad. 'And with everything Alex has been doing lately – coming to Zumba and looking out for lonely widowers, I think the least he deserves is a bit of apple crumble.'

'Yesss! Apple crumble,' I said.

'Does anyone in this house actually care what I think?' Dad sighed.

Nobody answered.

'Don't forget it's our turn to be on energy-saving mode, so everything needs to be switched off by 8pm, except for the essentials.' Mum got up to clear the plates.

'What parts of town are affected tonight?' asked Dad.

'Everything this side of Cherry Tree Lane,' Mum called from the kitchen. 'Us, Oak, Elmswood, Hazel, Blackthorn and all the connecting streets.'

'How are they going to know if we keep the Christmas tree lights on or boil the kettle?' Dad said.

'Oh, they check,' said Nanny. 'Mamie from Thursday Zumba had a two-hundred-pound fine slapped on her last week. They knocked on her door in the middle of the night.'

'There are patrols out.' Mum came in with some bowls of apple crumble and custard. 'So after eight, almost everything has to be switched off – no games consoles, microwaves, or computers. We can only boil the kettle once after eight, and we have to choose between the TV, or the wifi.'

'What?' We all looked up in horror, even Nanny.

'Only one or the other, after eight.'

'Son of a biscuit!' I said.

'Alex did a swear, Mummy,' Lauren shouted.

'Technically, he didn't,' said Mum. 'And stop trying to get him in trouble all the time.'

We all ate our apple crumble in peed-off silence, everyone annoyed about the prospect of choosing between possibly the two most important things in life.

'Will it be just like in the war, Nanny?' I said.

Everyone cracked up laughing, except Lauren who was still in a mood about the biscuit.

'I'm not that old, you cheeky monkey!' Nanny tried to look cross but was laughing as much as everyone else. 'Right, I'm going to give Mr McMonaghan a ring before the sirens start and we all have to go down to the bunker. Thanks for dinner, Judy.'

'You're welcome.' Mum looked surprised.

'Yeah, thanks, Mum,' I said.

'Shall we load the dishwasher?' Jess stood up and started piling up the empty bowls.

'If you guys take them into the kitchen, I'll load

the dishwasher while I'm making a coffee,' said Dad.

Jess and I took the dirty stuff out to the kitchen and then ran upstairs to message Dave and do our zombie make-up.

Jess was really into doing make-up, but not like the usual girl stuff. She liked painting horrific scars and Frankenstein-type things. She was pretty good at it, too. As a top secret agent, I thought it would be useful for both of us to practise, in case we ever needed to disguise ourselves. Mr Prickles woke up and started snuffling around, putting his nose into Jess's case and generally being adorable.

Jess started getting her kit out of the case and laying it out on the floor while I sat down and opened WhatsApp on my phone. As Mr Prickles cuddled up on my lap, I went into our group chat and started messaging, reading everything out loud to Jess and Mr P as it came through.

I typed: 'Sup D! *cheeky-poking-tongue-out-in-the-style-of-Miley-Cyrus emoji.*'

Dave is typing… 'Sup, m8 – is J at yours?'

'Yeah, her ma is out working so she's *sleeping emoji* here 2nite.'

Dave typing: 'I guess you want to know about the *envelope emoji*?'

'Yes!?????'

Dave typing: 'K, so I noticed there was no stamp on it. It had the postage printed on (franked). The frank was faded, but looked like a black octopus.'

'OMG!'

Dave typing: 'Also, every franking machine has diff code. Codes can be traced to exact machine at exact location.'

'We're getting vvvvvvvvvv excited here.' In fact, Jess had stopped getting her make-up stuff out and was kind of frozen with a sponge in her hand.

Dave typing: 'Hacking the system now. Should have address for you by tmrw *fingers-crossed emoji*.'

'Dave U R *geek emoji, cool emoji, 100 emoji*, legit.'

Dave typing: '*crying-laughing-face emoji.*'

'J says to say *kissy-face emoji, kissy-face emoji, kissy-face emoji*.' Jess punched me.

Dave typing: 'Will keep going and let U know when I get result. *Kissy-face emoji*.'

I looked at Jess. 'It's like breakthrough city up in here.'

She nodded. 'Let's try not to get too excited until we have an address and we know he's actually based there. Once we have that, we might have a chance of getting the evidence we need to put a stop to all this…' She dabbed at my face with some grey goo. 'But yeah, it feels like we're getting closer. Now, keep still while I do your eyeliner.'

15

The Apocalypse is Upon Us

I was desperate to plan our next steps, but Jess was right, it wasn't worth doing anything until we had something more concrete to go on. So we made each other look like zombies and ate snacks. When 8pm came around, I took one last look in the mirror before energy saving kicked in and the lights went out. I looked properly terrifying with rotting flesh hanging off my face, dark sunken eyes and blood smeared around my mouth. To make it festive, Jess had painted a holly leaf on one of my cheeks. I tried to do something similar for her make-up but she was mostly just a mess of grey and red. I put some glitter on her, too, for a Christmassy vibe.

As the lights in our house and everyone else's were turned off, my room grew creepily dark.

'Is it snowing yet?' I said.

'Soon,' Jess said, without even looking at the window.

I got up, cuddling Mr Prickles into my jumper, and peered out into the darkness to check for snowflakes and-slash-or people with octopus tattoos.

My street was dark, with only half the streetlights lit up.

'It wasn't long ago that all the lights were off because of The Storm,' Jess said, joining me at the window.

'It feels like ages, though. With all those power cuts before, you'd think there would be loads of spare electricity knocking about.'

'Yeah, it is weird,' Jess said. 'Have they told us why we need to do the energy-saving stuff?'

'Mum said something about it being colder than usual for this time of year, so people are using electric heaters more. And I guess there's all the Christmas lights.'

Jess suddenly looked at me with a gasp, and I knew it had hit us at the exact same time. 'The zombie party houses,' I said.

We both leant forward and peered out of the window towards Mrs Spires' house. Like every other house in the street, it was dark and quiet. There was a movement at her front door and we stared in silence for a second as we watched Mrs Spires come out of her house, shut the door behind her and turn to walk down the street.

A few tiny flakes of snow drifted down from the navy clouds.

'Where is she going?' I said.

'And why isn't she wearing a coat?'

'We have to follow her.'

'You mean sneak out? We'll get in so much trouble if we get caught,' said Jess, not taking her eyes off Mrs Spires who was getting further away by the second.

'I know,' I said. 'But we have to decide now.'

'Let's do it.' She stood up and we ran down the stairs as quickly and quietly as possible. Luckily for us, Lauren had decided to act out the whole of

Beauty and the Beast for Mum, Dad and Nanny. And she sang really, really loudly.

We grabbed our coats and let ourselves out of the front door, then legged it down the street after Mrs Spires. We put our coats on as we ran and I tucked Mr Prickles carefully inside mine (prickles facing outwards) so he wouldn't get too cold. Mrs Spires turned off on to Oak, disappearing in the dark patches between streetlights, then reappearing in the golden pools of light beneath the few that were lit. Other than us and Mrs Spires, the streets were completely empty. It felt like there was nobody else left in the world.

'I don't remember her being this fast,' I panted. 'She's proper power-walking.'

'At least running after her is keeping us warm,' said Jess.

'I hope wherever she's going, she gets there soon. We need to get home before anyone notices we're gone. If Mum finds out I've left the house, she'll go mental.'

'Look,' Jess hissed, pointing down one of the smaller roads that came off Oak Avenue. 'Someone else.'

I followed her gaze and could just about see

another lady in the distance. She was walking fast, like Mrs Spires, and she looked like she wasn't wearing her winter clothes either.

The sound of a door closing on my left made me turn again. A lady wearing leisurewear was leaving her house nearby.

'Wasn't that another one of the zombie party houses?' I whispered.

'Yeah, it was,' Jess said. 'This is seriously weird. Where are they all going?'

We followed the ladies, who were all heading in the same direction, trying to keep far enough behind that they wouldn't notice us or recognise us if they did. They were soon joined by Eileen and a man I didn't know – all of them walking fast and none of them wearing coats. The weird thing was that they all seemed so focused on getting wherever it was they were going that they didn't look around, they didn't say hello to each other and they didn't even check to see if any cars were coming before they crossed the roads.

As we reached Cherry Tree Lane, and looked beyond it to the other side of town, the world lit up. The houses on the opposite side of the road had been on energy saving the night before, so they were allowed to have their lights on.

'Maybe they're visiting friends so they can watch the *Antiques Roadshow*, or something?' I said.

'I think they need to be in the light,' said Jess.

'Not just the light,' I said. 'Remember at Mrs Spires' house? She had literally everything electrical turned on. And she did that inappropriate rubbing against the TV.'

'Don't forget the lamp,' Jess said. 'And the hairdryer at the leisure centre.'

'I know where they're going,' I pointed. 'The Pines.'

The snow had started to fall more heavily, whirling around us in the biting wind. Usually I would be fully into the snow situation, but this was distracting. We reached the corner of Cherry Tree Lane and The Pines and paused.

'Just a quick look,' I whispered. 'Then we have to run home.'

Jess nodded. Mr Prickles nodded too.

We crept around the corner and didn't have to walk far before we had a view of the whole road. It looked awesome as ever, with the lights twinkling, the reindeer nodding and a Christmas mini-train chuffing around the houses on a track pulling trucks full of presents. With the real snow it looked even more amazing. But we saw something else in The Pines that night. Something I will never forget, not for as long as I live. Me and Jess looked at the scene, eyes and mouths wide open for a moment or two.

'OMG,' Jess said.

'The Zumbies,' I said.

She looked at me. 'Zumbies?'

'Something this completely mental and horrifying deserves its own name,' I said. 'Once, they were dead in their leggings, but they were reborn. They stole through the night, ignoring everything but the desperate cravings they felt deep in their cores. They had only one need: the need to feed.'

'OK, Zumbies works, I guess, but the movie narrative is a bit clichéd.'

'The camera pans round to take in the terrifying scene,' I said, ignoring Jess's negativity. 'And settles upon the houses, lavishly decorated, like beacons of light in the dark winter night. A celebration of all that is good and joyful, and magnificently consumer-driven in this bleak, cold world. It would be the perfect Christmas picture, except for…' I paused for dramatic impact, 'The Zumbies.'

'I didn't know you knew so many adjectives,' Jess whispered, unable to tear her eyes away from the sight of the apocalypse unfolding in front of us.

'You underestimate me, as always, Jessticles,' I whispered back, gazing in shock and disgust at the houses and the decorations and the Zumbies. There must have been thirty of them. They were in people's gardens, surrounding their houses, rubbing themselves against walls strung with a million fairy lights, sitting astride animatronic reindeers and burying themselves in their synthetic fur. I saw Eileen riding the little train, using both arms to massage the sides of the engine so that she had to grip with her feet and was almost sliding off. The houses on The Pines all had their curtains tightly closed – they did that so people wouldn't try peeping into their living rooms. Lucky for them because it stopped them from seeing the horror on their front doorsteps.

'Is that Mrs Spires?' Jess said, pointing.

I took a step closer. Mrs Spires had wrapped herself around a life-size ho-ho-ho-ing Santa, hanging off his back like a baby monkey. As we watched her, with a mix of fascination and disgust, she started to lick its face.

'Oh no,' Jess said.

'Did you just do a sick in your mouth?' I said.

Jess nodded.

Mr Prickles squeaked.

'What do we do?' Jess turned to me, her face as pale as the snowflakes dancing around us. They were big now, like someone in the sky was plucking a Wampa and chucking clumps of its fur into the wind. They settled on the ground, forming a cotton-wool layer around our feet. They stuck in Jess's hair and eyelashes, hanging still for a moment, and then melting into tiny specks of water. Even Jess, with her frosty Elsa-ness, was too warm for the snowflakes to survive on. I watched as another flake melted on Mr Prickles' cute black nose. And then I watched as the snow fell on the Zumbies and stayed there.

'Look,' I said to Jess. 'The snow that lands on the Zumbies stays frozen.'

'It's settling,' Jess said. 'On people.'

A little mound was building up on Eileen's back as she rode the train around the track. Another lady was developing a snow crust, becoming a moving snowman.

'That's not right,' Jess said.

'I told you. Zumbies.'

'I can't stand to look at this any longer. Let's get home before your parents realise we've gone.'

We took a step backwards, and then something happened that nearly made my heart stop. What we thought was just one of the empty parked cars in the street turned on its headlights.

It was at the other end of The Pines, at the place where the road curled round in a semi-circle. I couldn't see who was in the driver's seat.

'Do you think it's Sean Darryl Lamb?' I said.

'Nobody knows we're here. We should go,' Jess said, as the sound of the car's engine being switched on rumbled through the quiet of the snow.

'Try to act casual,' I said. We turned and walked a few steps towards Cherry Tree Lane. We heard the car prowl forward, closing the space between us. I stopped walking and held Jess's arm to stop her, too. Behind us, the car stopped.

‘It’s going to follow us,’ Jess whispered.

‘OK. Forget casual,’ I said. ‘Let’s run.’

We turned on to Cherry Tree Lane and ran as fast as we could in the snow, which had turned from a gentle, drifting thing into a raging white monster. Luckily for us, the snow seemed to be making things even harder for the car. There was no way the driver would be able to see clearly through the windscreen, and the roads were icy, so he had to go slow. It gave us a chance.

I was about to cross the road so we could turn off on to Oak when I realised. ‘We can’t go home. Then they’ll know where I live and my whole family will be in danger.’ It was a horrible feeling, because all I wanted was to reach the safety of my house.

‘You’re right,’ Jess said. ‘So where do we go?’

We stood for a second, trying to decide, knowing Sean Darryl Lamb could be on us at any moment. I didn’t notice the blur of grey through the snow until Dexter was hovering right in front of our faces. Jess gave a single twitch, then started running down Cherry Tree Lane, pulling me with her. ‘Dexter said to go to the park and hide. He’ll try to help us.’

We sprinted along the road, our footsteps muffled by the snow. We could hardly see through the blizzard around us, but we knew the way. I'd been going to Rocket Park since I was a baby. I risked a glance behind and saw the car's headlights through the snow. It was getting closer. I tried not to think about what would happen if it caught us. Would Jess and I get snatched off the street and stuffed in the boot, never to be seen again? I switched on my speed boost, and my heart leapt as one of my feet slid out from under me and almost sent me flying. Jess reached out to grab me, and somehow I stayed upright.

'Finally, we have our epic chase scene,' I gasped.

'We just have to get to the end of the road,' Jess said. 'Then we'll turn right and take the shortcut to the park. The car can't follow down there.'

Underneath my coat I was pouring with sweat, but my face, fingers and toes were stinging from the cold. I could feel Mr Prickles being jolted up and down as I ran, but when I tried to use one of my arms to hold him still, I lost my balance again. I started to think that I wasn't going to make it. I looked back again to see the car was gaining – a few metres more and it would be clipping my heels. But then we suddenly emerged into the open space at the top of Cherry Tree Lane.

We turned right and made for the footbridge, knowing the car couldn't follow. I slowed a little and saw the car turn left – we had a few minutes breathing space.

'Do you think they'll drive around after us?' Jess said, struggling to catch her breath.

'I don't know,' I said. 'Maybe. Let's get into the park. We can cut through it and leave by one of the other exits.'

We slid down the slope to Rocket Park's main entrance.

'It's locked,' I said, rattling the gate and trying not to cry.

'Of course it is, it's December and 8:30pm. We'll have to find another way.'

We skirted the fence until we reached the place where it was lowest and the spikes on top of it were more rounded so we were less likely to get impaled.

'I'll boost you,' I said, kneeling down and linking my hands together.

'No way,' Jess said. 'I do NOT need a boost.'

I looked from the fence to Jess. Jess was fierce and brave, but she was also very small. There was no way she was getting over it with those teeny tiny legs. 'Go on, then,' I said.

She took a sort-of run up and tried to vault over it but barely left the ground. Then she gripped the bars and scrabbled with her feet but plonked back down in the snow.

'The car could be back any second,' I said, kneeling down again.

'Fine,' she sighed, putting her clompy boot into my hands – which hurt by the way – and she carefully swung one leg then the other over the fence and plopped down on the other side.

I pulled myself up with my hands and tried to grip the fence posts with my trainers. They were icy and slippery, and as I put my foot on the top of the fence to launch myself over, my foot slid and I lurched forward. I tried to spin in mid-air so that if I crashed, I wouldn't squish Mr Prickles, but I ended up landing awkwardly, my ankle twisting with a zap of pain.

'Quick,' Jess said, reaching out a hand to pull me up. 'I see headlights in the distance.'

I tried to stand but my ankle gave way beneath me with an even bigger stab of pain. I couldn't get up.

'Alex, come on!' Jess shouted. She was being buffeted by the wind and I could barely see her frightened zombie face through the clouds of snow.

I was so cold, and so tired and too afraid to even look at my ankle, knowing there would be a shard of broken bone sticking out of it or something. So instead I curled up in a ball and lay on the snowy grass.

'What are you doing?' she said. 'We have to move, now!'

'I can't,' I said. 'I'll probably never walk again. Take Mr Prickles and go without me. Save yourselves, I'll only slow you down.'

'Don't be stupid, we're not leaving you here. You'll freeze to death!'

'I'll build myself a snow nest,' I said.

'You won't have a chance if Sean Darryl Lamb finds you,' Jess shouted. 'Now get up, you idiot.'

She grabbed my arm, really hard, and pulled me up. She was scarily strong. 'We're in this together,' she said.

'I won't make it out, though.'

'Then we'll hide.'

16

Primary Targets

We looked around us. The Rocket Park was huge and had lots of different areas. There was a skate park on the right, and then some tennis courts with a café next to them. On our left, a river ran all the way down one side of the park, towards the other end where the sprinkler park, which was locked up for the winter, stood next to the playground. The playground had all the usual stuff in it, including a rocket-shaped climbing frame, which is how the park got its name. Right in the middle of the Rocket

Park was the bandstand, which was like a gazebo on a high platform. I don't really know what the point of it was, but the naughty kids liked to hang out on it, with bags of energy drinks and boxes of nuggets. There weren't many lights in the park, but the snow had made everything brighter.

'We could hide in the playground – in the cubby hole under the rope bridge, by the spinners,' Jess said.

'But look at the snow on the playground – it's perfect and flat. Even in the dark they'll be able to see our footprints.' A good agent always considers the terrain. 'We can cover our tracks better on the grass. I know a place in the bushes by the river.'

'It's darker there, too,' Jess nodded. 'Come on, I'll help you.'

She put her arm around me and we staggered across the snowy grass, using sticks to mess up our tracks. We climbed over a low wall, being careful not to disturb the snow on top of it, which would give our hiding place away, and pushed through the trees and bushes until we found the hollow. We crawled in, one at a time and tried to make ourselves invisible. I'd hidden in there loads of times during games of hide and seek, so I knew you couldn't see it from the park. The bush was thick, so there was no snow underneath it, and we had shelter from the wind.

With the park on one side of us, and the river on the other, we were as hidden as we were going to get. And just in time. On the other side of the river was the road. Cars couldn't drive into the park so we were hoping the car would just forget about us and drive on. But a light from the road grew brighter and brighter, lighting up the inside of our bush, and making the glitter on Jess's face glint when she turned her head towards the sound of the engine. The car passed us, moving slowly, and we held our breath. But it stopped.

'It must have seen our footprints going into the park,' Jess whispered.

'It?' I said. 'Are you saying the car is actually alive and making its own decisions?'

'I didn't mean…' she started.

'Because that would be awesome. It could be like a robotic lifeform or something. Do you think it's a Decepticon?'

A car door slammed shut, not too far away from our hiding place, quickly followed by another.

'Two doors,' Jess whispered.

'I guess Sean Darryl Lamb has an accomplice.'

We held our breath and strained our ears. For a few minutes all I could hear was the sound of the wind gusting through the trees, making branches creak and groan and broken twigs drop to the ground. There were rustles in the undergrowth around us – goodness knows what was in there with us, but it made me extra glad that I had Jess and Mr Prickles with me.

My mouth was as dry as a camel's tail and the more I tried not to think about it, the worse it got. I wondered how long we'd have to wait until we felt it was safe enough to leave.

And then we heard the voices.

A man said, 'They definitely came in here.'

'You take the left side and I'll take the right,' a woman answered. 'Be rapid and thorough. We can't risk being seen.'

Through the tiny gaps in the bush, we could see a shaft of light moving through the dark, not far from where we were. It swept across the grass, back and forth, getting closer with each zig-zag.

I nudged even closer to Jess, the smell of damp earth mixing with the mildly chemical smell of our make-up.

The sound of some weird atmospheric music cut through the wind and snow. It was all violin-y and sounded like it ought to be the soundtrack of a movie with dark elves in it. For a second I thought I was hallucinating, but then the woman said a bad swear and the searchlight stopped sweeping. She was just a few metres away from us.

'Sir?' she said sharply, as the music, which must have been her ringtone, stopped. 'Affirmative, we observed the test subjects leaving their residences and proceeding to a local road called "The Pines".'

A pause.

'That's the one, Sir. I'm afraid the situation has escalated faster than we anticipated. It won't be long before people start to notice, and the whole operation will be compromised. We need all of Black Octopus on high alert.'

Another pause.

'That's affirmative, Sir. I recommend urgent action to deal with the test subjects. Full clean-up. I'll alert the geo-engineers.'

Jess squeezed my hand, and I squeezed hers back. This was bad.

'No, Sir, we're no longer at that location. We weren't alone in observing the test subjects.'

Pause.

'It looked like two Caucasian youths: a male and a female. When they registered our presence, they fled. We pursued the youths in the car, but they entered a park so we're now proceeding on foot.'

Pause.

'Visibility is poor due to the weather conditions, Sir. And the youths were wearing masks or some kind of face-paint.'

Another pause.

'While some aspects, such as height and approximate age certainly fit the profiles, I cannot confirm one hundred per cent that the youths in question are our primary targets.'

Me and Jess both gasped at the same time, then shoved our hands over our mouths when we realised the sound our gasps made were loud enough to give us away.

There was a second of silence.

'I'll call you back, Sir. I may have something here.'

The glare of the searchlight turned in our direction.

I sat as still as I could, holding Jess's hand and

trying to use the force to slow my heartbeat and stop my bladder from leaking the juice I drank at dinner time all over my pants.The light got closer. She was right in front of our bush. She was going to find us.

I tried to think fast. There were two of us, three if you counted Mr Prickles, and two of them. Our only hope was to get away before the man came back from the part of the park he was searching. But my ankle was throbbing and I knew I wouldn't be able to run.

She swung a leg over the wall.

Panic built.

She pushed through the shrubs in front of our hiding place. This was it.

I felt a movement in my coat, and Mr Prickles crawled out of the top, rolled into a ball and dropped onto the ground. My hand shot out to grab him, but he ran off, straight towards the lady with the scary elf ringtone. He crashed through the bush as loudly as he could, huffing and squeaking.

The lady swore again. 'Just a stupid hedgehog.'

I held my breath, praying to Yoda that she wouldn't hurt him. Then a voice called out from quite a long way away.

'Over here! A flock of birds has been disturbed by the far exit.'

'On my way,' she said. 'We need to contact clean-up – the houses must be hit tonight.' The lady ran off and everything went quiet. I was desperate to get out of the bush to see if Mr Prickles was OK but Jess held me back. I counted to one hundred and twenty in my head. There was no sound but the rustle of the park around us. The wind had grown calmer, almost like its panic had passed when ours did. It made me feel a bit braver knowing the weather was on our side.

'Ready?' I whispered to Jess.

'Yes. Slowly, though. Check the coast is clear before you go bolting out into the park.'

'Do you take me for some kind of amateur?' I whispered, crawling through the opening and actually forgetting to look for bad guys, because I was concentrating on looking for Mr Prickles.

It was too dark to see much, but there definitely weren't any humans in sight. Or any hedgehogs.

'Do you think she took him?' I said, as Jess emerged from the bush behind me. I was crawling around, looking under plants and rooting around in the snow.

'Just a sec,' she said. 'I hear him, he's calling.' She twitched for a moment, then smiled. 'It's OK, he followed the woman to make sure they'd left and he's on his way back. They've gone out of the far exit. We can escape.'

'Thank fudge,' I said, standing up and then remembering that I'd fatally wounded my foot.

'I'll help you walk,' Jess said. 'But only if you do something about that snot on your face. It's one of the most disgusting things I've seen in my life and it's making me feel sick.'

'More disgusting than Mrs Spires licking Santa?' I said, using my glove to wipe it away.

'No,' she shuddered. 'That was way worse.'

'He's coming!' I could see Mr Prickles scurrying across the snowy grass. As I bent down to pick him up, I felt tears stinging my eyes. 'You saved us!' I cuddled him into my coat again. 'You were so brave, but please don't do that again.'

'He says it was no big deal,' Jess smiled, putting an arm around me and helping me walk back to the low part of the fence.

Getting back over wasn't easy, but I put the pain to the back of my mind and focused on getting the heck out of there. We took the back way home, so if the car retraced the journey down Cherry Tree Lane, they wouldn't see us.

We'd been gone much longer than we'd planned and I half expected to see Mum, Dad and Nanny out looking for us. But the house was quiet and dimly lit. I could hear Lauren still singing inside.

'Charming,' I said. 'They didn't even notice we left. What if we'd been abducted and murdered? Lauren gets all the attention.'

'Let's just be glad we're not going to get in trouble,' Jess said. 'Where are the keys? We can sneak in and they'll never even know we went out.'

'The keys?' I said.

'Yeah, you know, the keys to open the door?'

I tapped my pockets just to double-check what I already knew. I gave Jess my best cute puppy-eyes face. 'Um ... oops.'

17

Recruiting Dexter

In the end we had to ring the doorbell and pretend to my parents that we'd gone outside to play in the snow. They weren't happy, but it was the best we could think of. I told my mum I'd slipped throwing a snowball at Jess and twisted my ankle, so Mum was distracted, fussing over that. And, as it turned out, it wasn't broken or bleeding, just a bit puffed up.

'You might have to give Zumba a miss tomorrow,' Mum said.

'No way, I'm not skipping Zumba. We have the flash mob coming up soon and I need to get the routine down.' I also needed to spy on Da'Shon and the Zumbies and make sure Mum and Nanny were safe. And I also really enjoyed it, but nobody needed to know that.

'So you will walk again after all?' Jess snorted.

'Fine, but you'll need to take it easy,' said Mum. 'Bedtime in an hour.'

Me and Jess went upstairs and she started wiping off her zombie make-up while I fed Mr Prickles and put a pile of straw on the floor for him. He liked to drag it into his little cubby hole to make it comfy-cosy.

'So much to talk about,' Jess said. 'I don't even know where to start.'

'Did that woman's voice sound familiar to you?' I said. 'I'm sure I recognised it.'

'Yes, I thought so too! And was the man Sean Darryl Lamb? And who was she on the phone to?'

'She kept calling him Sir, so it was either her boss or a Victorian schoolteacher.'

Jess laughed, which made me relax a bit. I hadn't realised how tense I still was from seeing the Zumbies, the chase, the hunt, and everything we'd overheard.

'Let's think it through,' Jess said. 'They were watching the Zumbies but she called them "test subjects" on the phone.'

'Like what Taran said about the animals he did experiments on.'

'So they're Zumbies because of what someone has deliberately done to them?' Jess said. 'That's nuts.'

'Not just someone, Jess: Montgomery McMonaghan. It has to be.' I started cleaning my face with some wipes from Jess's pack.

'That's who she was on the phone to in the park,' Jess gasped.

'Assassin Tight-Face!' I shouted.

'What?'

'That's why we recognised her voice – she was the woman with Montgomery McMonaghan outside the lift at the SPARC lab when we were escaping with the animals. What was her name again? Maybe it's Maybelline?'

'Evangeline! Oh god, you're right. So he *is* behind all this.'

'Of course he is,' I said.

'But what's he been doing to them to, you know…'

'Kill them, then turn them into electricity-guzzling Zumbies?' I said. 'We must have missed something.'

'There was the other stuff she said on the phone.' Jess started packing her make-up stuff back in the case.

'Yeah.' I'd been putting off thinking about it, but we had to face facts. 'They've been watching the Zumbies, but they've been watching us, too.'

'She called us "primary targets".'

'The net is closing in. We're going to have to go off grid.'

'Off grid? Really?'

'It's the only way. It's how they do it in the movies.'

'So you're going to give up your iPhone?' Jess snapped the clasp on her case shut.

'Whaaaa?'

'If you're going off grid, that means no laptop, tablet or phone.'

'I thought it meant you had to live in a shack in the mountains and grow a beard?'

Jess sniggered. 'Like you could grow a beard. But, yeah, the shack part sounds right.'

My phone buzzed in my pocket. 'It's Dave,' I

said. 'He has an address from the envelope code! And if I gave up my iPhone, I wouldn't have that incredibly useful piece of information.'

'We have to stick around anyway,' Jess said. 'Do you remember what the woman said about taking urgent action against the Zumbies.'

'Full clean-up.' I nodded.

'So, what's the plan?'

'We have an address for Montgomery McMonaghan junior now. We confirm that's where he is and then we find a way in.'

'What will we do once we are in? We need evidence about what he's doing to the ladies from Zumba, and we don't even know what that is. And, as always, we're running out of time. What do you think they meant by "a full clean-up"?'

'They don't want anyone to notice the Zumbies, so they're either going to turn them normal again, or get rid of them.' We both knew which of those scenarios was the most likely. 'And it's something to do with G.O. engineers.'

'Which are?'

'Obviously they are Genetically-modified Octopus engineers. They're creating monster octopuses with a high tolerance for electricity and wrinkly skin, to devour the Zumbies.' Jess was so slow, sometimes.

'Yeah, I don't think that's it, but we need to find out. This is bad.'

It *was* bad. And I hated that Mum and Nanny were mixed up in it. If Montgomery McMonaghan attacked the Zumbies, there was a good chance that half my family would be caught in the crossfire. 'Let's use Zumba class to look at them all, proper closely, to see if we can find more connections, other than just the Zumba, and that they all have a crush on Da'Shon.'

'We need to know how Da'Shon is connected. He's not being honest. He's sneaking stuff into their food and he had the octopus on his shopping list. He could be working for McMonaghan.'

'He could be,' I said. 'But I really hope not. My gut keeps telling me he's a good guy.'

'Mine too,' Jess said.

A tapping on the window made me jump.

'They've found us,' I said. 'Take cover!' And I dived under my bed.

'It's Dexter,' Jess said. She opened the window and he flew into my room.

'Thanks for causing the diversion earlier and leading Montgomery McMonaghan's minions away from us,' I said, pulling myself back out from under the bed, as casually as possible. 'You saved us.'

Jess started twitching. 'He followed the car as far as he could, but lost it when it sped up just outside Cherry Tree Lane.'

'How did he know we were even out?' I said. 'Don't get me wrong, I'm super glad he was there, but it was a surprise.'

'He's been keeping an eye on us. He's worried about Miss Fortress and wants us to help him end Montgomery McMonaghan.'

'Awesome.' This was exactly the kind of bad-A talk that got me excited. 'Listen, Dexter, we want to help Miss Fortress, too, and we have a lead on Montgomery McMonaghan. Will you help us?'

Dexter cocked his head and watched me with his beady eyes. He looked like such a bad-A, strutting around, even with two toes missing. He was totally loyal to Miss Fortress, and we needed him if she was ever going to be happy again.

Jess began to judder.

'He says that if our plan is to take down

Montgomery McMonaghan then he'll do anything he can to help,' Jess said. 'That geezer is Thames scum and deserves to pay.'

'Can you tell us anything about him that we don't already know?' I asked. 'Maybe something Miss Fortress has told you?'

Jess twitched away. 'She only told him what she told us, really, about them working together and then him starting to change when his mum died. There's one other thing, though. Dexter thinks there was another person in their family – someone who lived with them. A child, or a pet. Definitely female because Miss Fortress cries about it sometimes and says how she misses her.'

'What happened to the child-slash-pet?' I said.

'All Dexter knows is that Montgomery Mcmonaghan took her and hid her. Miss Fortress has no idea where she is or if she'll ever see her again.'

'Oh, man, that's so sad.'

'Yet another reason to stop that son of a…'

'…Biscuit. Definitely.' I turned to Dexter. 'We have a new lead – an address where we think McMonaghan might be based. Will you check it out for us?'

Dexter nodded, waited only for us to give him the details, then flew back out of the window into the night.

Soon after, Mum called Jess downstairs for bedtime – she'd made her up a bed in the living room. I gave Mr Prickles a kiss, then got into bed myself. I knew I should try to sleep, but I couldn't stop the thoughts wheeling around my head in a horrible, muddly clash – like my little sister and her friends at roller disco. It had been a crazy day, visiting old Mr McMonaghan, sneaking out to follow the Zumbies, running for our lives. Tomorrow was going to be a big day, too. Tomorrow we had to work out exactly what was going on with the Zumbies, before it was too late. What I didn't know then was that tomorrow would bring even more confusion and turn the mess we were in into a full-on disaster.

18

OMG MY EYES!

Nanny went to Zumba early the next morning, to meet up with some friends. Sometimes they get a bit rowdy, but nothing could have prepared me for what I saw as I limped up the ramp at the leisure centre. I stopped dead, and tried to make sense of the horrific scene in front of me.

'What's up with you?' Jess said, as she caught up with me. Then she saw what I was seeing. 'Oh no. What is going on?'

The outdoor pool, which had sat abandoned

since the summer, with piles of snow around the its edge and water that must be as cold as our evil teacher Miss Smilie's smile, was full of people laughing, splashing and swimming. And not just any people – it was the entire Zumba class, Nanny included.

'Tell me I'm hallucinating again,' I said.

'I'd love to,' Jess said. 'But that really is your nanny in a swimming costume, Alan in tiny trunks and all the other Zumba ladies in swimsuits and bikinis.'

'My eyes,' I said, trying to tear them away from the sight before me.

That was when Mum caught up. 'What on earth are they doing? They'll catch pneumonia!'

'They look like they're enjoying themselves,' said Jess.

'It's madness and it has to stop,' Mum said, walking carefully to the edge of the pool. 'Come out at once, all of you. You'll make yourselves ill!'

'The water's lovely!' Nanny shouted back. 'Bracing! You should join us.'

'It wasn't very long ago that your nanny said you'd never catch her in that pool,' said Jess.

'I know. It's wrong. So. Very. Wrong. And not

just because I really don't want to see them in their swimwear. It isn't even just the Zumbies, it's all of them. What's happened to make them act this way?'

'Maybe,' I saw Jess side-eye me. 'Maybe the rest of them are starting to turn.'

'Into Zumbies?! My Nanny, a Zumbie? It can't happen!'

'Then we have to find out what is going on and stop it.'

Mum was shouting at all of them to get out of the water.

'Jess. Look at their arms,' I said.

'They all have those posh fitness bands,' Jess gasped. 'It was never that obvious before because they weren't...'

'...All mostly naked,' I said. 'It's the bands. It must be.'

'We need to get our hands on one,' Jess said.

'And we need to get Nanny's off her before she turns full Zumbie.'

'Let's see if they still have them on reception.'

We turned away from the disturbing scene in which about thirty people, who were old enough to know better, were pulling themselves out of the icy pool, and walked up the ramp. As the doors swooshed open, we were greeted by the sight of Angel taking all the fitness bands out of the display and putting them in a cardboard box.

'What are you doing with those bands?' I said.

'Packing them away. We're not selling them anymore,' Angel said, in her usual bored way.

'Why not?' I said.

'Not sure,' she answered. *Lie.*

'Is there something wrong with them?' I said.

I watched her face. She was very good at looking bored and being inconspicuous, but she obviously knew a lot more than she was giving away.

'No. Just not for sale anymore.' *Lie.*

'Are you sure?' I said, 'Because my nan wears one, and if there's something wrong with it, I need to know. It won't do anything to her, will it?'

'No,' Angel said, finally looking up from her box. My ear rumbled and the strong swimming pool smell was for once covered by something much worse. She stared at me. 'What sort of thing are you talking about, anyway?'

I didn't know how much Angel knew, and I didn't know how much Angel knew I knew, but it would definitely be best to make her think I didn't know very much, and that I definitely didn't know that she knew more than she seemed like she knew.

'Dunno, give her a rash or something?' I said. 'She wears it all the time and she has delicate old-lady skin.'

'It shouldn't give her a rash,' Angel said, and that, at least, was true.

'So, the fitness bands are safe?' Jess said.

'Sure.' Angel shrugged, picking her phone off the counter and starting to tap away. And, yeah, she was lying again.

The doors swooshed and Mum walked in. 'Good morning,' she said. 'Three for Zumba, please.'

She was just paying for our passes when the doors swooshed again. I turned around to see Mr McMonaghan dressed in a polo shirt and some tracksuit bottoms. He smiled and waved when he saw me and Jess.

'Your grandmother convinced me,' he said.

'How wonderful,' Mum said. 'You must be Mr McMonaghan? I'm Alex's mum. The others are just, um, getting changed, so if you follow us we'll show you where to go. I'm so glad you've decided to try Zumba.'

They walked off ahead, so Jess and I had a chance for a whispered conversation.

'It's so nice that he's come,' I said. 'But now we've probably put him in massive danger.'

'We didn't know. We'll just have to keep him safe.'

'So, new plan,' I said. 'We do Zumba, watch Da'Shon, watch the Zumbies and try to perfect the new routine, because I'm struggling with that middle section when we have to jump-kick with the swirly arm movements.'

'Hopefully your nan will have some clothes on by then.'

I shuddered. 'At some point today, I will steal her fitness band, and then we'll get it to Miss Fortress tomorrow, so she can examine it.'

'Dexter should report back soon about Montgomery McMonaghan's lair.'

'Jessticles, I love that you used the word "lair".'

'And then we'll plan an infiltration.'

'Jessticles, I double-love that you used the word "infiltration".'

'This danger has been around us for weeks, and

things are only getting worse. We need to get serious if we're going to stop it, and if that means I have to become more like you…' She looked at me. '…Like a better version of you, then that's what's happening.'

My grinchy heart grew three sizes bigger. 'Welcome to the dark side.'

19

Under Arrest

Da'Shon arrived with swag, like always, and started the class. The Zumbies were on fire. They knew every step and performed it perfectly, they had bounce and rhythm and all those other things that Da'Shon said we were supposed to have. None of them gave anything away about their antics of the previous night. Mr McMonaghan was doing his best, when he wasn't being embarrassed, and he looked like he was really enjoying himself. It should have been awesome, but my brain was chaos, like there were tornadoes full of sharks and lava and yodellers swirling around it. I couldn't focus. I missed half the transitions, went left when I was supposed to go right, and shimmied when I should have slid. Jess was even worse, but that was standard.

'Everything all right, my fellas in the back?' Da'Shon called out.

'I have a bad ankle,' I said. 'And Jess is being Jess.'

'Well, don't stress, my friends, just enjoy it and the moves will come together.'

That's when four police officers burst into the room. Everyone gasped and fell silent, waiting to see what was happening.

'Sean Darryl Lamb, I'm arresting you on suspicion of attempted murder and theft. You do not have to say anything. But it may harm your defence if you do not mention when questioned something which you later rely on in court. Anything you do say may be given in evidence.'

I looked around the room, expecting a sinister super-criminal to de-camouflage himself and emerge from the yoga mats. But the police were standing in front of Da'Shon.

'What are you talking about?' Nanny stepped

in. 'His name is Da'Shon and he would never do those things.'

'Da'Shon isn't his real name, love,' the police officer said. 'And he has previous.'

'Don't you "love" me,' said Nanny. 'Who's he supposed to have attempted to murder, then? And what's he supposed to have stolen?'

'For starters, a defibrillator from this leisure centre,' said another officer. 'He used it in a class on one of his victims...' He looked down at his notebook, '...an Eileen Crabbe, then failed to return it.'

'I'm not a victim,' Eileen shouted. 'He saved my life and takes care of my fitness and wellbeing, as well as brightening my sad, lonely days.'

We all looked at Eileen.

'We're not at liberty to discuss the full nature of the charges,' the first police officer said.

'I'm not a victim,' Eileen said. 'He saved my life.'

'Oh no, she's doing that repetitive Zumbie thing,' I said to Jess. 'We need to stop this from getting out of hand.' I stepped forward and patted Eileen on the arm. 'You're upsetting her,' I said to the police officer in my angry, but not so angry you'd want to arrest me voice.

'We'll be out of your way in one minute, lad. Let's get him in the van.'

'No!' Nanny said, standing in front of Da'Shon. 'I want to hear it from him.'

'Me too,' said Alan.

'And me,' someone else shouted.

'Let's give him a chance to speak, shall we?' Mum looked at Da'Shon with her most worried face.

'Da'Shon,' I said. 'Is your real name Sean Darryl Lamb?'

'It is,' Da'Shon said, looking at the floor.

'And have you previously been convicted of a crime?'

'When I was younger,' he said. 'I got in with a bad crowd and we broke into an old lady's house to steal a DVD player. But when we were there it felt all wrong, so I told my crew to leave it. It turned into a fight, the others ran off and I got caught.'

Everyone gasped.

'Seriously?' I said.

'I swear.' He wasn't lying. 'I went down for it, as I deserved, and did my time. When I got out I swore I'd use my life to help people, especially people who are a bit vulnerable. I wasn't upfront about it because I thought I wouldn't be given a chance.'

'Then why have you been putting substances in their food?' the second police officer asked.

'It was high-dose vitamins, all healthy stuff,' said Da'Shon. 'But I got it at a discount from a friend so I kept it quiet.'

'So, you'd never do anything to hurt any of us?' I said.

'Hell, no. You people are my family. You're all I have.'

Everything he'd said was the absolute truth, and though I didn't need my ear to tell me that, it was good to have confirmation.

'There's still the matter of the missing defibrillator.' Angel was standing in the doorway. 'Explain that.'

'I can't,' Da'Shon said. 'I don't know where it is.'

'Time to go,' the police officer said, and they led him out of the door.

The moment the door closed behind them, everybody went mental.

'I don't believe it,' Eileen was saying. 'He saved my life!'

‘This is outrageous and it won’t stand,’ Nanny shouted. ‘We’ll fight for his release.’

‘We can’t do the flash mob without him,’ said Alan. ‘We need him, poor chap.’

‘Has anyone seen the defibrillator?’ Mum looked around at everyone. ‘It must have gone missing. If we find it, we can clear Da’Shon’s name.’

Everyone was talking at once and everyone had something different to say, but not a single person in that room believed Da’Shon was guilty.

‘You think he’s being set up?’ Jess said to me.

‘That’s exactly what I think. Montgomery McMonaghan is smart and he always has a get-out plan. I don’t know exactly how Angel is involved, but she’s constantly sending messages on her phone and she’s in the perfect position to incriminate Da’Shon.’

Jess closed her eyes for a second. ‘So this is all part of the Black Octopus Operation Clean-up.’

‘Exactly.’

Everyone kept talking, trying to think up ways to get Da’Shon back. Nobody had the heart to carry on dancing.

Mr McMonaghan stood at one side of the room, listening, but not saying much.

'This must all seem a bit nuts,' I said. 'Sorry we invited you here, but it's not normally like this.'

'I'm not sorry,' he said. 'This is the most excitement I've had on a Sunday morning for years.'

'Da'Shon is a good guy, honest,' I said.

'He must be to have everyone here so passionate about helping him. We all make mistakes in our lives. If I'd have done a better job with my son, he might not have chosen such a bad path.'

'What do you mean?' Jess said. 'I thought he was clever and successful.'

'He is.' Mr McMonaghan looked sad. 'But I don't approve of some of the choices he makes. He's single-minded, you see, and doesn't let anything get in his way when he's decided what he wants.'

'And what does he want?' I asked.

'To find out everything he can about the illness that led to the death of his mother. She was always so healthy, apart from the odd cold, but when the illness took her, it was like she got thirty years older in the space of a couple of months. He thinks he can find a cure.'

'To help other people?' Jess looked surprised.

'No, to help himself. To keep himself fit and young, and to make millions from selling his cure to those who can afford it.'

'That's awful,' I said, because I knew Jess was too angry to speak.

'And it's my fault, really. I worked a lot when he was growing up, and I was firm with him. It was different back then, you know. Most dads didn't get as involved with their children. I could see that he wanted my approval – that he wanted me to be proud of him, but I had no time for it.'

'He made his own choices,' said Jess.

'True enough, but he might have made better ones if I'd done right by him.'

The crowd in the studio started breaking up and Nanny came over to us.

'We're all going for a coffee, Mr McMonaghan, would you like to join us?'

'I'd love to,' he said. 'And please call me Monty.'

They left the room together.

Da'Shon's arrest was all anyone talked about for the rest of the day. It wasn't until after dinner that I finally got to chat to Nanny alone. I'd thought up a hundred plans for stealing her fitness band, or tricking her into giving it to me, but in the end I decided that the best way would be to tell the truth, or at least part of it.

'Nanny,' I said, sitting next to her on the sofa. 'I need to ask you something important.'

'Of course, Alex. What is it?'

'It's about this.' I tapped her fitness band.

She put a protective hand on it and looked worried. 'What about it?'

'Well, I think these bands might be what's causing people to collapse.'

'That can't be right. Since I've been wearing it, I've never felt better.'

'That's part of it, though, Nanny. They make you feel better but they can actually really hurt you,' I said.

'How do you know this?'

'That's the problem, I don't know for sure, but I have a really clever friend who'll be able to examine it and tell us exactly what it does.'

'So, you want to borrow it?' I could see that Nanny was reluctant, even after what I'd told her. It was like her version of the *The Lord of the Rings* ring. I watched her face carefully to see if she was turning into Gollum and made a note in my mind to keep track of how many times she said 'precious' over the next few days. Time to pull out the big guns.

'Also,' I said. 'If we can prove that these bands are dangerous, it will help us to get Da'Shon out of trouble.'

'Really?'

I nodded. 'I think so. Please, Nanny?'

'In that case, you take it for as long as you need it.' She peeled it off her wrist and gave it to me. 'But once you're done, if it's not going to kill me, I'd like it back.'

'Of course, Nanny. Thank you. I love you.'

We had a cuddle on the sofa for a couple of minutes, until it was time for Mum to drop her home.

20

Triple M

The next day, me and Jess gave Miss Fortress the fitness band and explained some of what had been happening over the past week.

She looked horrified. 'Why didn't you come to me, again? I could have helped.'

'You've had other stuff on your mind, Miss. We didn't want to bother you,' I said.

'And we didn't want to bring up Montgomery McMonaghan until we knew whether he was involved.' Jess sat on the edge of a table, swinging her legs.

'And now we know.' Miss Fortress stared at the fitness band like it was a bomb about to explode. She'd opened it up and had a look inside. 'At a guess, I'd say that the band sends electrical pulses through the nervous system.'

'Like electric shocks?' Jess said.

'Tiny ones, probably undetectable to the wearer. But with prolonged use, it could interfere with the circuitry of the heart.'

'Which would explain the collapses,' I said. 'But how did the Zumbies come back to life?'

'Possibly the device has an emergency setting that kicks in when it can no longer sense the wearer's heartbeat, administering a stronger shock to restart the heart.'

'That actually makes sense,' I said.

'But what about all the freaky things they've been doing? The repetition and the being amazingly good at Zumba?' said Jess.

'I imagine the repetition is to do with the brain rebooting, maybe glitching a little as it does and resorting to memory and repetition. That would make them excellent at remembering the dance routines too. It's possible that the device is performing fairly efficiently in the job it's supposed to be doing, keeping the wearers healthy and active.'

'And the rubbing of electrical things?' I said.

'I imagine those are cravings. After a time, the band doesn't satisfy the wearer's need for the electrical pulses, so they seek them elsewhere.'

'Which explains why we have a power shortage in Cherry Tree Lane,' said Jess.

'It's a whole world of wrong,' I said.

'It is,' Miss Fortress sighed. 'But if the device does work as we've discussed, then it's also a thing of genius. A few more tweaks and he could actually crack it.'

'You don't happen to know what a G.O. engineer does, do you, Miss?' I said.

'Geo-engineers are concerned with intervening in the Earth's natural systems – trying to control the climate and weather, for example.'

'So, it's "geo", not "letter G, letter O",' Jess said. 'That makes a lot more sense.'

'I assume so, unless there is a whole branch of science that I'm not aware of, which is extremely unlikely.'

'But how would geo-engineers be involved in cleaning up the Zumbies?' I said.

Jess shrugged. Miss Fortress frowned. It seemed we still had a lot of unanswered questions.

We sat in silence for a few minutes, listening to the tick-tock of the clock and the distant sound of children playing outside. I could hardly remember what it was like to be able to run around with nothing to worry about except winning Fortnite.

'Once we're done with this mission,' I said. 'Let's give ourselves a few days off over Christmas, just to, ya know, enjoy some downtime, eat nice food, open presents ... that sort of thing.'

'Sounds good to me,' said Jess. 'What will you do over Christmas, Miss Fortress?'

Miss Fortress blinked a couple of times. 'Ah, well, I'll be busy working on some new projects.' She took a mouthful of coffee, opened her desk drawer, unboxed a chocolate orange and started hitting it on her desk with the ferocity of a raging bear. The foil split and bits of chocolate flew across the classroom, but she didn't stop smashing it until it was literally in tiny pieces. Then she took the destroyed foil off, and put a handful of chocolate shards in her mouth.

Jess and I just stared at her. 'Are you OK, Miss?' I said.

'Of course.' She did a weird laugh that sounded more like a sob. 'Whack it, don't tap it.'

It wasn't until afternoon break the following day that we finally heard back from Dexter. Me, Jess and Dave were sitting on the Reflection bench, reflecting about what we wanted for Christmas, when he swooped out of the sky and landed next to us.

'Hey, Dexter,' I said. 'Did you find it? Is he there?'

Jess twitched while I jumped up and down incredibly patiently, saying helpful things like 'hurry up' and 'tell me'.

Eventually Jess looked up. 'We've found the base. He's been there every day since Dexter's been on watch and only a handful of people come and go.'

'What did you say the building was listed under, again?' I asked Dave.

'MMM Research and Development.'

'Mmm, research and development – could he be trying to create the world's tastiest snackfood?' I asked.

'I read it as triple M, rather than mmm,' said Dave. 'I thought it might be a combination of his and his mother's initials – Maggie Montgomery McMonaghan.'

'You are a genius, Dave,' I said. 'Now, how are we going to get in?'

'Dexter actually had an idea about that,' said Jess. 'Every day at 10am, a van pulls up from Cherry Tree Aquatics.'

'Isn't that the shop by the garden centre that sells pond and aquarium supplies?' said Dave.

'Exactly. Dexter has managed to see that Montgomery McMonaghan has a giant aquarium in his office. The Aquatics people come every day to clean and maintain the tanks and check on the health of the fish.'

'Brilliant work, Dexter,' I said.

'He also overheard that there's a delivery of new fish being taken from Cherry Tree Aquatics to the aquarium tomorrow morning.'

This was very exciting. 'So if we can somehow get Bob in the delivery going to Montgomery McMonaghan's aquarium tomorrow, he can spy for us, help us to find the evidence we need and the day will be saved!'

'That's what Dexter was thinking,' said Jess. 'Great plan, Dexter.'

'I have to congratulate myself on putting together such an amazing team of operatives,' I said.

'Of course you do.' Jess rolled her eyes.

'I've done an awesome job. Well done, Agent Alex.'

'You all make a great team,' Dave smiled.

'You mean *we* all make a great team, David. We couldn't go on without the cyber-master that is Darth Daver.'

'Thanks, Alex,' Dave said. Jess rolled her eyes even harder.

'Dexter, do you think you can keep an eye on Bob while he's in the aquarium? Watch through the windows and pass messages back and forth – that sort of thing?'

Dexter nodded.

'You da boy,' I said. 'Now we just need to find a way of getting Bob into that delivery.'

21

BIG News

After school, I asked Mum if she'd take me and Jess to Cherry Tree Aquatics.

'What on earth for?' Mum said.

'I would have thought that would be obvious, Mum. We need to get a Christmas present for Bob and Elle. Fish deserve Christmas, too, you know.'

'You've left it a bit last minute.'

'Because I wanted to wait until I'd found the perfect gift. And now I have, at Cherry Tree Aquatics. Fish deserve perfect gifts, too, you know.'

'Do we need to go right now?' Mum looked at her cup of tea and chocolate Hobnob on the coffee table.

'Yes. It's what all the fish are into right now, and I don't want them to run out before I get there.'

'Fish are into things?' Mum said.

'Of course. Fish deserve to enjoy popular trends that everyone will have forgotten about by the summer, too, you know. I'm starting to think you're a bit fishist.'

Mum sighed. 'Let's go, then.'

'Jess!' I called into the kitchen, where Jess was stashing Bob in her schoolbag. 'We're going!'

'Coming!' She ran into the hallway with her coat on, ready to go. She gave me a nod as soon as Mum wasn't looking. That meant Bob had agreed to help, as long as we let him watch *Home Alone* when he got back. I'd told him that was a good movie about being part of a big family and what it's like to have kids.

Fifteen minutes later, we were at Cherry Tree Aquatics.

'You can wait in the car, Mum,' I said, slamming the door shut in case she had any ideas about coming in with us. We walked into the shop.

From the outside it looked like a shack where homeless people might live, but on the inside it was really cool. It was hot and dark, and there were shelves and shelves of tanks full of different fish.

'OK,' Jess said. 'The order for MMM Research and Development must be in the back area, which according to Dave is behind that door.' She nodded at a door marked 'PRIVATE', which stood slightly open, just behind the counter.

'And there are only two people working – Raph and Lexi. So that must be Lexi on the till, but let's scope out the premises and make sure we have eyes on Raph before we run the distraction.'

We skulked around the store, checking for CCTV cameras, other customers, and the elusive Raph, who was nowhere to be seen.

'He must be out the back,' I whispered. 'We need to get both him and Lexi into this corner so one of us can go through the PRIVATE door, find the right tank and plant Bob inside.'

'Right,' Jess nodded. 'Bob's in my bag, so I'll plant him.'

'Why don't you hide behind that shelving over there – it shouldn't be hard because you're...'

'... Very small, I know.' Jess sighed.

'I was going to say because your hair's like that yellow coral over there – the stuff with all the tangly tentacles that if a fish swam into, it would never find its way out of. Anyway, I'll go make a scene.'

'It's what you do best,' Jess said, and she hid behind the racks.

'Good afternoon to you,' I said to Lexi at the till. 'I'm interested in buying an aquarium. Could you help me, please?'

'Sure,' she said, 'But just to let you know, we're closing in five minutes.'

'This won't take long,' I smiled. 'Shall I show you what I'm thinking of?'

I led Lexi away from the counter, past where Jess was hiding, and into the furthest corner of the shop.

'I like the look of that tank, up there.' I pointed to the top shelf. 'Could you please get it down so I can see.'

Lexi frowned. 'That's going to be too heavy to get down on my own. I'll have to call my colleague and get some ladders.'

I heard her sigh as she walked back to the

counter, poked her head around the STAFF ONLY door, and said, 'Raph, we have a customer who wants to look at the Exotica Deluxe 40-litre tank.'

I couldn't make out exactly what Raph said in response, but I'm pretty sure there were some swears in there.

'I know,' Lexi said. 'If you help it will get done quicker.'

I heard some scraping, and then Raph appeared in the doorway with two ladders and a moody expression on his face. I gave him a cheerful wave. As soon as Raph and Lexi were busy in my corner, climbing the ladders and then working out how to get the tank down safely, Jess darted into the back room. In the end it took quite a while for Raph and Lexi to get the tank off the shelf. It was obviously heavy and they had to balance at the same time, so there was a fair bit of huffing and under-breath swearing.

Just as they finally got it down and slid it onto a lower shelf, Jess came out of the staff area and gave me a nod.

'How much is it?' I said to Lexi and Raph.

Lexi looked at the price label. 'It's £199.99.'

'Oh, I don't have that much. I'll just take this fish food and plastic coral, please. It reminds me of my friend's hair.'

I don't think Raph and Lexi liked me very much, so I paid quickly and walked outside to where Jess was waiting.

'All good?' I said.

'He didn't like being in with the strange fish, but he was pretty brave about it.'

'I hope his journey tomorrow is OK,' I said. 'And who knows what it'll be like in Montgomery McMonaghan's aquarium. It's a dangerous mission.'

'Yeah, it never gets easier leaving him in places. Let's hope this is the last time.'

We had to wait until afternoon break on Wednesday to hear from Dexter, who met us in the usual place at school. He didn't stay long, just had a quick word with Jess and then flew off.

'Bob is in place,' Jess said. 'The aquarium in Montgomery McMonaghan's office is enormous, Dexter says – it takes up a whole wall. There are loads of fish in it, but it's clean and the fish are well looked after.'

'That's something, at least. He should be safe and comfortable.'

'The most dangerous thing in the tank is an octopus,' Jess said, all casually, like she was telling me what she'd eaten for lunch.

'Shut. Up.' I said.

'Err, why?'

'He actually has an octopus?' I jumped off the bench. 'What am I saying? Of course he has an octopus – he's a super-villain! This is the coolest thing ever.'

'Well, if you like that, you'll be even happier to know that it's a poisonous octopus.'

'Oh my god, you're messing with me?'

She stared me down.

'You're not messing with me. Montgomery McMonaghan has a poisonous octopus and I never knew until this very moment, and it's one of my favourite-ever things to find out about a person.'

'It's a blue-ringed octopus,' Jess said. 'It has a very poisonous bite. Oh, and she's called Suki, apparently.'

'After school, I am going to google the heck out of blue-ringed octopuses. I need to know everything.'

Jess sighed and Dave cracked up laughing.

'Wait. She won't hurt Bob, will she?' I said.

'No, Dexter says most of the fish avoid getting too close to her, and she's given plenty of food, so there's no reason for her to go after the fish.'

'Awesome.'

Then Jess said a bunch of other things, but I didn't really listen because I was thinking about the octopus. I didn't listen to any of my literacy lesson either, because I was thinking about the octopus, and then I spent the whole time between school and Zumba finding stuff out about the octopus. They live in the Pacific and Indian Oceans, and they look all normal and yellowish until they get angry and then they totally hulk out. But they don't turn green, they get bright blue rings all over their skin. And then they bite. Their bite contains a toxin that paralyses people, and can kill them!

Isn't that the coolest pet you've ever heard of in your whole entire life?

When we walked into the Zumba studio, I'd almost forgotten that Da'Shon wouldn't be there. Nanny and Mum hadn't forgotten, though – they'd been making plans.

'Is everyone here?' Nanny said, looking around with her strict face on and scaring everyone into shutting up. The whole class was waiting, even Mr McMonaghan had come. 'We're here today, not to have our regular class, but to hold a council of war. For the sake of appearances, let's stand in formation and play our music so that it appears to any observers that nothing is out of the ordinary.'

'Now I know where you get your overly-dramatic streak from,' Jess whispered to me as we shuffled into place. Mum turned the music on, not as loud as we normally had it, but loud enough to make the whole conversation difficult to hear.

'Alan, will you serve as lookout?' Nanny said. Alan nodded and took his place at the door. He held the remote control for the speakers in his hand.

'If I turn the music up, dance like nothing untoward is happening,' Alan said.

'As you all know, Da'Shon has been wrongly accused of committing multiple criminal offences,' said Mum. 'But we're not going to let him go down without a fight.'

'My wonderful grandson is already taking steps to find out the truth behind the charges, so we're hoping to clear Da'Shon's name,' Nanny said.

Everyone turned and smiled at me, so I gave them a heroic wave.

'But, in the meantime, we need to become a force to be reckoned with. We need to raise awareness of our campaign.'

The music suddenly blared out, five times louder than it was before, and we all started to dance, trying to pick up the routine at the right point in the song, bracing ourselves for someone to come prying into our private meeting. But the volume went down almost straight away.

'Sorry, false alarm,' Alan shouted. 'My hand slipped – I get sweaty when I'm nervous.'

'There will be press at the flash-mob event, so we're going to use it to make sure everyone knows that Da'Shon is innocent,' said Mum.

'We have these…' Nanny crouched down to open a big cardboard box.

The music suddenly blared again, so we started to dance. The door opened and Angel walked in and it occurred to me how strange it was that she'd suddenly started taking such an interest in our Zumba class.

She signalled for the music to be turned off, looked bored while she waited for quiet and then said, 'We've had the details of the flash mob. We're lucky to have businessman and philanthropist

Montgomery McMonaghan opening the festivities and making a generous charitable donation on our behalf. The leisure centre would like you to know how important it is that you attend.'

I looked at Jess, and then we both looked at Mr McMonaghan the older, who was trying to cover up the fact that he was doing some kind of smiling with tears thing.

Angel gave Alan a piece of paper, then left the room.

Alan passed the bit of paper to Nanny, who, for whatever reason, seemed to have become the Winston Churchill of the situation.

'This is it,' she said. 'We go to war in the Rocket Park on Saturday and do our bit to make sure justice is done. We'll be wearing these.' She opened the cardboard box and pulled out a T-shirt with a massive picture of Da'Shon's face on it. It said "Free Da'Shon – The Cherry Tree Lane 1".'

Everyone cheered.

'We'll Zumba like we've never Zumba'd before,' Alan said.

'Damn right, we will,' Nanny said. 'We'll Zumba and we'll win.'

22

I Face My Fears

Dexter reported in to us on Thursday and Friday, bringing messages that he'd managed to get from Bob through the window of Montgomery McMonaghan's office. As far as we could tell, Bob was doing brilliantly. The trouble was, he could only pass Dexter limited information. We'd have to wait until we broke him out of triple M to get the full lowdown on Montgomery McMonaghan's plans for world domination. And that led us to our next problem.

'Dexter says Bob has Montgomery McMonaghan's computer password.' We were sitting on the Reflection bench and Jess had just juddered through a quick conversation with him. 'And Bob's seen him analysing the data from the fitness bands.'

'Can you hack Montgomery McMonaghan's computer?' I asked Dave.

'No way.' He shook his head. 'I'm sorry. His cyber-security is tighter than anything I've seen before. He has better firewall software than the government.'

'I love how putting "cyber" in front of any word makes it cooler. Cyber-security. Cyber-warfare. Cyber-Alex.'

'Can we please focus?' Jess huffed.

'Right,' I said. 'So the only way we can access files on Montgomery McMonaghan's computer is to log on to his actual computer?'

''Fraid so,' Dave nodded.

'OK, that means one trip to get Bob, get the evidence we need and get out,' I said. 'McMonaghan will be opening the flash mob at the park tomorrow, so this is our chance.'

'On a Saturday, there probably won't be many people around, so it's a good time to sneak in,' said Dave.

I nodded. 'We know that Montgomery McMonaghan is dangerous, so we don't want to risk a confrontation. Not that I'm scared or anything. This mission is about stealth.'

'So how will we do it?' Dave asked.

'Luckily, I…' I started to say, but was interrupted by Jess.

'Actually, this time *I* have a plan, and I'm fairly confident it will work.'

As much as I really wanted to follow my plan, it was so exciting to see Jess finally embracing being an agent that I didn't have the heart to stop her. And then when she told us the plan, I had to admit that it was sick.

'There are lots of things that could go wrong,' Jess said.

'But if everything goes right, it'll be perfect,' I said. 'Besides, it wouldn't be any fun if there wasn't a significant chance of failure and death.'

During this mission, for the first time since we got our powers, me and Jess had done some proper sneaking around. It made me feel daring. It made me feel exposed. After all, if we got caught, it wasn't just our lives that would be in danger – it could also mean the removal of all Xbox privileges, permanently.

I told Mum that I was leaving early for the animal sanctuary the next day, and she believed me. I felt bad about it, but sometimes agents have to make tough calls, and this was for her own safety. We'd actually cancelled our shift – between infiltrating Triple M and taking part in the Zumba flash mob, we had no time for clearing up animal poo. I gave Mum an extra hug before I left that morning, just in case.

The snow from the weekend had all melted, and it was a different kind of cold – less skin-stinging, more deep and damp. The sky was thick with clouds the colour of pencil lead.

Jess was waiting for me on Cherry Tree Lane.

'Are you sure this part of the plan is necessary?' I asked. It was the part I was dreading most – the part that had kept me awake half the night.

'Certain,' Jess said. 'Stop being ridiculous.'

Dave appeared around the corner with a big smile. 'Who's being ridiculous?'

'Alex, obviously,' Jess said.

'We talked about this,' Dave said, in a kind and patient way. 'It's going to be alright.'

'But last time...' I started to say, before Jess rudely interrupted me.

'Alex, everyone gets sickness bugs. It happens all the time. There's no way of knowing where you got it from. Now shut up. It's here.'

The C17 bus rolled to a stop in front of us. I took my last gulp of clean air, pulled on the spare gloves that I'd brought with me specially, and got on, trying not to touch anything.

'I hate the bus,' I said, after we'd walked to the back and sat down.

'Oh, really?' Jess said. 'I would never have known that.'

My ear did a little fart, but to be honest, it couldn't make the smell any worse than it already was. The windows were steamed up and I imagined all the used breath swimming around me. Ugh. I closed my eyes. 'Distract me. Let's go through the plan again.'

'We all know the plan, Alex,' Jess said. 'It will all be fine unless someone catches us.'

'Fear not, Jessticles – I brought my weapon just in case.'

'You're not actually going to use a weapon on someone, are you?' Dave said.

'Probably not, but they don't know that.'

'Let's see it, then,' Jess said.

'OK. Prepare to be overwhelmed by its destructive power.' I pulled it carefully out of my pocket and held it in the palm of my hand.

Jess cracked up.

'What?' I said.

'Alex,' Dave said. 'That looks like...'

'It's a laser,' I whispered.

'And what do you think it does?' Jess said. 'Because I've seen these before and I know exactly what they're capable of.'

I was a bit disappointed that she didn't seem impressed. 'It blasts things,' I said.

'It doesn't.'

'It seals wounds so people don't bleed out.' I looked at it hopefully.

'Nope,' Jess smirked. 'Give it here.'

'OK.' I handed it to her. 'But be careful.'

She grabbed it, pointed it at my chest and flicked the on switch. I braced myself for pain and death, but there was nothing. I looked down expecting to see a hole where my heart should be, but there was just a tiny red light shining on my coat.

'It's a laser pointer, Alex,' Jess said. 'People use them as cat toys.'

I'm not going to lie; it was pretty humiliating.

'Oh look, we're here,' I said. And I even risked pressing the bell, just to get myself out the awkward laser situation. 'Let's go!'

MMM Research and Development was a five-minute walk away from the bus stop, but I didn't mind. It was nice to be able to breathe fully again.

'Time check?' Jess said.

'Ooh, get you, taking charge,' I said. 'It's 9:37.'

'Let's move. We need to be concealed by 9:50 at the latest.'

'Sir, yes sir,' Dave saluted. And that made me laugh.

MMM Research and Development looked very different from the SPARC lab we'd visited a few weeks before. That had been an enormous glass building on an industrial estate. This looked more like a fancy house.

It was bigger than a normal house, but smaller than a mansion. It looked old, though, with plants climbing up the walls and wrapping around the window frames and wooden beams decorating the outside. It was set back from the main road, with a massive driveway covered in tiny pebbles. The wooden front door was double-sized, and had a shiny knocker, rather than a doorbell.

'Are we sure this is the place?' Dave whispered.

'Definitely,' Jess said. 'We need to hide by the back entrance.'

'Across the crunching pebbles of doom?' I said.

She nodded. She'd spent a long time talking to Dexter and working out the layout of the buildings, so she knew what she was doing.

I'd like to say we tiptoed across the gravel, but it's not really possible to tiptoe on gravel, so actually we just ran for it, hoping that nobody would hear us. We crept around the side of the house until we could see behind it. It opened up on to a sort of paved courtyard, with two other long buildings that looked barn-like running opposite the house and to the left. Jess pointed at a dark corner between the two buildings. We hid, and waited.

At 9:58, a van with the Cherry Tree Aquatics logo on the side scrunched over the gravel and parked on the right side of the courtyard. I recognised Lexi in the driver's seat, and Raph when he opened the passenger door and jumped down in his Cherry Tree Aquatics polo shirt. He walked round to the back of the van, opened the doors and pulled out some long tube-shaped carrying cases with handles. Lexi followed, grabbing two heavy-looking trunks.

'Quick,' Lexi said, 'or we'll miss the buzzer.'

Raph swore and broke into a jog towards a door at the back of the main house. He put down a box and put his hand on the handle.

At exactly 10am, I heard a buzzing sound and Raph pushed the door open, letting Lexi go in ahead of him, then pulled in the case and watched the door swing shut behind him.

'I hope Bob understood the plan,' I said, as we waited again. Waiting is the worst. It makes you feel like your bones are going to explode.

At 10:07, the door opened and Raph appeared with one of the cases. He looked around to see if anyone was watching, and then used the case to prop open the door. Then he walked across the courtyard to the gravel driveway and round to the back of the van.

This was our chance. We ran from our hiding place to the open doorway and into the house, being careful not to trip over the case holding the door. We were in a short corridor leading to a reception area, which was unmanned due to it being the weekend. We sprinted across and bundled behind the reception desk, making sure that all our arms and legs were out of sight, especially Dave's which were like a Sith giraffe's.

We heard the door slam, and Raph walked back in with the case he'd used to hold the door open, and another even heavier-looking one that was labelled 'Retrieval and Removal'.

'False alarm.' Lexi's voice called from somewhere upstairs. 'It's not dead after all.'

Raph muttered something and rolled his eyes, letting the heavy retrieval case drop to the wooden floor with a crash. I smiled to myself. It had been Bob's job to pretend he was dead, and he'd obviously done a convincing job. Raph stomped up a metal spiral staircase.

Again, we waited.

At 10.25, Raph and Lexi clunked down the stairs again with all their gear. They walked down the corridor, chatting about some party they'd been to the night before, then we heard the door slam shut and everything went quiet.

'Time to go to work,' I said, standing up and swinging my bag over my shoulder.

'You've been waiting to say that, haven't you?' Dave laughed.

'Yes,' I said. 'For the film.'

We ran up the stairs and into a huge room, with lots of sofas around coffee tables and floor-to-ceiling bookshelves full of brown, leather-covered books. There must have been thousands of them.

'Why do super-villains' libraries never have normal books in them?' I said. 'I know they like to have the evil-books-from-the-crypt vibe going on, but you'd think they'd at least have a copy of Harry Potter.'

At the far end of the room was a polished wooden door with patterns carved around the edges. 'That must be it,' Jess said. We ran towards it, focusing on speed rather than stealth. We wanted to get in and out before anyone came and found us. I turned the handle on the door and pushed it open.

The rest of the house looked like it had come from one of those TV shows that my mum liked, where people wore bonnets and drove around in horse-carts; Montgomery McMonaghan's office was totally different. There was still lots of wood, but it was newer and simpler, with no patterns or carvings. There was also technology, including a wall of TV screens like all super-villains have, where you could watch thirty different shows, or just one show stretched across the whole wall. There was a desk with a black leather chair, more bookshelves, and glass cabinets full of stuff.

What really made me stare, though, was the wall that wasn't a wall – it was the biggest fish tank I'd ever seen. It was the Buckingham Palace of fish tanks.

'How do we get into it?' I said.

'There should be a door hidden on the right, behind the shelves that will lead us to the aquarium and holding tank.'

'Yes! Hidden door. Another super-villain hallmark ticked off the checklist,' I said.

'Alright, Dave – you take the computer,' Jess said, pointing to Montgomery McMonaghan's desk. 'The password is...'

'Wait, let me guess,' I said. 'Is it "IAmTheBringerOfDoom"?'

'No, it's...' Jess looked at her left hand where she'd written it in purple gel pen. 'MoMcSaLa95.'

'Well, that's disappointing.' I hurried over to the tank and scanned across it.

'Bob's right there,' Jess pointed.

'Oh yes, sure,' I said. 'That's who I was looking for – my old friend, Bob. Not the octopus.'

Obviously, my ear farted, and Jess sidestepped away from me, with a dirty look and started fiddling with something on one of the bookshelves.

Bob was also giving me a dirty look.

'Sorry, Bob,' I said. 'I'm really happy that you're OK, and thanks for doing such a good job. It's just I'm super-excited about the octopus because I've never seen one in real life.'

'Bob said Suki is in her cave, at the bottom left corner of the tank,' Jess called out from where she was still fiddling with the bookshelf.

I looked at a small rock pile on the floor of the tank. It was a heap of grey stones with a dark hole in the middle, surrounded by brightly coloured coral. The thing was, it only came up to my knees.

'It can't be,' I said. 'It's not possible.'

'What do you mean?' Dave said, without looking up from Montgomery McMonaghan's computer.

I looked at the cave hole. 'It's so small.'

'How big do you think the octopus is, Alex?' Jess said.

'I did my research, thank you – I know exactly how big it is. It's six to eight…' I didn't know what the " sign was in words, so I made it with my fingers instead.

'And how big is that?' Jess sniggered.

'Like the size of a double-decker bus,' I said, feeling suddenly far less certain than I had earlier. 'Or at least the size of a large tiger.'

Jess and Dave started laughing at the exact same time, and couldn't even stop for long enough to let me know exactly how long six to eight" was. I was starting to think I might have been mistaken in my original estimation. From the corner of my eye, I saw a wobbly orange thing, jiggling about. I looked across to see Bob shaking in the water.

'Great, even the goldfish is laughing at me,' I said.

'And he never laughs,' Jess spluttered.

Bob wiggled his way across the tank to the entrance of the little cave, peered in and then quickly swam to a safe distance.

Jess twitched for a second. 'Suki's coming out to see you.'

I stared at the cave entrance, too excited about

meeting Suki to care about the mission. I know, I know: it wasn't very professional of me. But a poisonous octopus? That was the stuff of dreams.

'What's she like?' I whispered to Bob. 'Is she all sinister, with a razor-sharp, dark humour and the kind of confident air that only comes from knowing that you're superior to everyone else in the room?'

'Got the door lever,' Jess said, and the shelves slid to the side allowing access to the tank.

'Forget that, Jess,' I said. 'Come and translate.'

'How are you getting on with the computer, Dave?' Jess called.

'I'm in, just searching for the files,' Dave called back.

'OK, we have a few minutes.' Jess walked over as the tip of a tentacle slid out of the cave and curled around the rocky entrance. She jerked about as Bob spoke to her, and then she started laughing again.

'She's basically the opposite of what you just said,' Jess snorted. 'She's always happy, in a Disney princess cliché kind of way. She's super-sweet and, because she hasn't got an octopus family around her, she just wants everyone to love her.'

'Oh.' I watched another octopus arm weave out of the hole, followed by another, and another. They were covered in suction pad things and looked so cool. I couldn't believe they belonged to something that wasn't a bad-A.

Jess moved closer to the cave, as the head of the octopus, which was a sandy, yellow colour and about the size of a Christmas pudding, emerged from the darkness, its black eyes staring up at me and Jess.

'Hi, Suki.' Jess waved. 'I'm Jess and this is Alex. It's great to meet you.'

Suki darted out of her cave and jet propelled herself upwards so that she was level with Jess's head. Fish scattered around her, hurrying away so that she had a sort of buffer zone around her at all times. None of them wanted to get too close.

Jess twitched for a bit as Bob bobbed nervously, and Suki flexed her arms which were addictively watchable – the way they constantly coiled and waved.

'What's everyone saying?' I hissed at Jess.

'Bob said he's been trying to persuade Suki to give up some secrets about Montgomery McMonaghan, but she refuses.'

'Why?'

'Because he's the only family she has. He talks to her and tells her she's beautiful, and she likes that, it makes her happy.'

'Do you mean a bittersweet kind of happy, that makes the shadows in her soul seem even darker?'

'No, I mean happy, happy. Like, "he loves me, yay!" happy.'

Suki started jetting around the tank, her tentacles streaming out behind her with awesome power and general bad-A-ness.

'Have you ever seen her get angry, Bob?' I asked.

Jess jiggled, then smirked in an annoying way. 'He hasn't. None of the fish here have. Nobody has ever seen her angry, she's just…'

'Happy, happy. Yeah, I get it.' I sighed.

'For example,' Jess said, clearly enjoying herself. 'Would you like to know what she's saying right now?'

'Looks like you're going to tell me and shatter my dreams even more,' I said.

'I am,' Jess nodded. 'She's saying, "weeeeee!" as she whooshes around the tank.'

'Of course she is,' I sighed. 'It's great to meet

you, Suki. I hope one day to see you give yourself to the dark side.'

'Got it!' Dave said, looking up from the computer. 'The data files from the fitness bands are all here. Come look.'

We ran over to the desk and peered at the screen. There was a list of names, which included all the Zumbies we knew about, and more too. As my eyes scrolled down, I saw a name that made me feel sick. 'Nanny,' I said.

'Click on Mrs Spires' name, Dave.' Jess pointed. 'Let's see what information there is on her and if it's enough to incriminate Montgomery McMonaghan.'

I don't know what I'd been expecting, exactly – maybe a few numbers and a couple of pie charts – but the data on Mrs Spires went way beyond. There were charts with multiple rows and columns, full of figures and notes. And there was a long graph, with a line that went up and down like on the heartbeat monitoring machines you see on hospital TV shows. It had markings across the bottom to show when the fitness band gave out the electrical pulses and how strong they were, and we could see exactly how this affected her heart. We skipped through to the day Mrs Spires died, and there her line was flat.

'This is it!' I said. 'This is the evidence we need!'

'Well, aren't you quite the crack team?' A steely voice came from the doorway. I didn't need to look up to know who it was, but when I did (in slow motion so it would look better in the movie), I saw Montgomery McMonaghan himself, watching us with a smile on his face.

23

The Scuff of Hope

'Jess and Alex, at last,' he said. Then he looked at Dave. 'I don't believe we've met. I'm Montgomery McMonaghan. Would you like to tell me what you're doing on my private computer?'

'Actually.' I stood as tall as I could, which is really quite intimidatingly tall. 'It's "Alex and Jess", not "Jess and Alex".'

'So glad you finally made it,' McMonaghan said. 'You've been interfering in my business so much over the past few months, I've been looking forward to discussing it with you.'

He was wearing the face of someone who *knows* stuff – someone who holds all the cards and has a spare pack hidden up his sleeve. I tried not to let my fear show on my face.

'You don't seem surprised to see us here,' I said.

'I'm not an easy man to surprise,' he laughed. 'I like to keep ahead of the game.'

I assessed our situation. He was blocking the only exit that I was aware of. There were three of us and one of him, but I was pretty sure he had bodyguards who would be somewhere close by, probably just behind the door that was our only escape. I needed time to think. We had to keep him talking.

'How did you know we'd be here?' I said.

'I'd be only too happy to tell you about that, as soon as your friend steps away from the keyboard.' Montgomery McMonaghan fixed his glinty eyes on Dave, who was frozen mid-click. Dave looked at me. I nodded. He moved his hands back and rested them on the desk.

'I see we all understand each other,' McMonaghan said. 'Superb.' He clapped his hands loudly and sharply, making me jump. 'Now then, where to start? How about with Jessica Joan Lawler?' He turned to Jess and took a step towards her. 'Eleven years old, an only child who lives with her mother, a social worker. Attends Cherry Tree Lane Primary School where she is a slightly above average student with a talent for art and the social sciences.'

'So, you know a couple of things about me. Am I supposed to be scared?' Jess glared at him.

'Rebellious, moody, brave. A fighter wherever she sees injustice.'

'Ooh, he's making you sound like Batman, Jess,' I said. 'That's so cool.'

'And there's another special thing about Jess Lawler,' McMonaghan said. 'She has a rare gift in her ability to understand animals.'

My mouth went dry and I stared at McMonaghan as he took another step forward. Jess didn't flinch.

'And so the question I asked myself is...' McMonaghan smiled '...was Jess Lawler born with this talent, or did she acquire it by other means?'

'Funny you should ask that,' I said. 'We can't decide whether it's because she slipped in some toxic slime one time, or because she touched the glowing rock that fell from space.'

'And Alex Sidney Sparrow.' He turned to me.

'Ten years old. Lives with his mother, father and younger sister Lauren – his grandmother often stays with them too. The perfect middle-class, suburban family...'

'You wouldn't say that if you saw them arguing,' Jess snorted.

'Also, my name's Alex Danger Sparrow, if you don't mind,' I said. My ear did a little fart.

'And here's the intriguing thing about Alex,' McMonaghan said. 'Wherever he goes, an unpleasant odour follows.'

'That's just rude,' I said. 'My middle name might be Danger, but I still have feelings.'

'Which raised further questions, because he doesn't look more unclean than any other child his age...'

'Err, thanks?' I said.

He narrowed his eyes at me. I got the feeling he didn't like to be interrupted. 'What could be the cause of this smell? And was it linked to the way this boy seemed to be able to get beneath everyone's skin?'

'So far this is a really boring origins story,' I fake yawned. 'I thought you were going to tell us something interesting.'

His head snapped round to look at me. 'Oh, it's an interesting story, alright. It's the tale of two children.' He walked over to Jess and leant down so that his face was chillingly close to hers. 'Two children who were given incredible gifts – gifts that could only have been discovered by one of the greatest minds of our time. And this time I'm not referring to myself. There's someone I've been looking for, for a long, long time, and something tells me you know exactly where I can find her.' He stepped in front of me, in his perfect suit, smelling of crashing waves and expensive sports cars.

And then he said something that filled me with horror.

'And that's why I brought you here today.'

'What?' I said. '*We* found *you*.'

He laughed then – a strangely high-pitched giggle that made him sound deranged. 'Oh bless,' he said, ruffling my hair. 'Is that what you think?'

It is what I'd thought but I was starting to realise I might be horribly wrong.

'I've been watching you for weeks. I needed to know more, so I decided to test you. I planted a series of clues – breadcrumbs if you will – to lead you to me, to this place, to this moment.'

All the clues that had seemed too convenient, really had been too convenient. They were planted. We'd thought we were being so clever, but he'd been one step ahead of us the whole time.

'You were never opening the Zumba flash-mob event, were you?'

'Of course not,' he laughed. 'I wanted to make sure you'd be here so I told you I'd be somewhere else. Don't worry, I've sent a special gift to the park, to compensate for my absence. I've observed you all along: at the cricket club, the leisure centre, on the streets of Cherry Tree Lane. I knew you'd locate my father and use the Christmas card to find this place.'

'You used your own father?' Jess said, looking more cross about that than any of the rest of the stuff he'd said.

'It's good to finally have a purpose for him.' McMonaghan shrugged.

Something in the way he said it made me want to know more. 'Don't you care about him at all?'

'No, why would I?' he said, and my ear rumbled. 'He's never cared about me. Now, here's the situation you find yourselves in...' Obvious subject change. 'Waiting outside that door are two of my most trusted and formidable security team members. You cannot leave this room and you cannot beat me.'

He'd been playing us. He was too clever and too powerful – how could we win against someone so untouchable?

And then he made a big mistake. He put his hand on the side of Jess's face and stroked it. 'Tell me where she is.'

At the same time, Dave and I both jumped towards him, but not before Jess had whacked Montgomery McMonaghan's hand away and stomped on his shiny, shiny shoe. 'Never touch me, you creep!'

He stayed rooted to the spot, although it looked like it took a huge effort for him to not retaliate. His hand dropped to his side and he sort of hissed.

I glanced down to see that Jess's boot had left a big, dirty, scuffed footprint on Montgomery McMonaghan's shoe. Even though we were in heaps of danger, it made me smile. He wasn't untouchable. It was like the scuff of hope.

And just like that, the seed of a plan zinged into my mind.

'You think you know everything,' I said. 'But you don't.'

'I'm confident I know everything I need to know. I've played the game perfectly, moving all the pieces into position so that I will be victorious.'

'Well, we know a few things too,' I said. 'We know about the fitness bands, about you wanting to find the key to eternal youth in a classic super-villain cliché.'

'You won't get away with that,' said Jess. 'You messed with the old ladies too much, and soon everyone will notice.'

'I've put someone else in the frame for any erratic behaviour displayed by the ladies in the Zumba class.' He smirked. 'And who really cares about a group of old dears with nothing better to do with their lives but prance around making everyone embarrassed?'

'Hey, that's my mum and my nanny you're talking about,' I said. 'And, actually, the rest of them are awesome too.'

'And why did you choose Da'Shon to take the fall?' Jess said.

'He had an unfortunate past – just another

mindless thug who's better off in jail anyway. With a well-placed ally in the perfectly named Angel, and some other assistants – it was almost too easy.' McMonaghan shrugged. He really didn't care about anyone.

'He's not a thug,' Jess said.

'And he taught us to free ourselves through dance,' I said.

'Now he's helping me to make a clean break from the unfortunate effects of this experiment.'

'And what about all the evidence that points to you? The bands, the data, us?' I stared him down.

'I'm glad you asked about that.' He did a full smile, his extra-white teeth gleaming like Venom in the Spider-man movie. 'All of the evidence will be destroyed. Including you.'

I'm not going to lie – I was really scared. There was nothing Montgomery McMonaghan wouldn't do to get his own way. The next few minutes could be the difference between life and death for me, Jess and Dave.

So I laughed. Jess and Dave looked at me like I'd lost it.

'Something amusing you?' McMonaghan asked.

'Heck yes,' I said. 'As I mentioned earlier, there are things you don't know.'

'Such as?'

'I have a weapon of immense power in my pocket,' I said.

'Alex,' Jess whispered. 'We talked about this!'

'What kind of weapon would this be?' Montgomery McMonaghan clearly didn't believe me.

I put my hand in my pocket. 'It's a weapon that could destroy everything in this room – all of your nice stuff.'

'Go ahead, destroy it. There's nothing in here that can't be replaced.'

'What about your wall of flat screens?' I said. 'Or your books that look like Egyptian artefacts?'

He shrugged. 'Nothing I'd miss.'

'What about your giant aquarium and fish collection?'

'They're just fish – there are millions of them swimming around in the oceans of the world.'

I looked at him and then pointed at Suki. 'And what about your octopus? Surely she's special to you.'

He looked over at her, sitting at the bottom of

the tank, perfectly still, watching the scene playing out in front of her. 'She is a beauty, but I could have a replacement choppered in by the end of the day. Maybe something even more beautiful, perhaps a bit bigger.'

My heart leapt as he said it. 'There's something else you don't know. We have a man on the inside.'

He actually looked a little surprised, just for a second. 'And who is this inside man?'

'I'll show you,' I pointed to the tank. 'Meet Agent Bob.'

As McMonaghan turned his attention to the tank, I gave Dave a tiny nod and rolled my eyes down to the computer. Then I took a few steps towards the aquarium. 'Agent Bob has been watching you. Among other things, he gave us your computer password.'

'A spying fish? How fascinating,' McMonaghan also moved closer to the tank. 'Not that knowing my password is going to help you get out of this room.'

'He's also been building relationships,' I said. 'With your fish, and with your octopus.'

'How delightful.' He clapped his hands. 'I hope they won't miss him too much when I get him out of that tank and squash him under my shoe. Or maybe I should just flush him down the toilet?'

Jess gasped. Bob eyeballed me. I hoped this was going to work.

'Bob has something he'd like to say to you,' I said. 'He's learnt a lot lately … haven't you, Bob?' I turned to him. 'The things we've been talking about for the past couple of weeks. Why don't you explain it to everyone?'

'Oh yes, I should love to hear the thoughts of a goldfish – it's an experience I shall probably never have again. So let's hear what he has to say before I kill him.'

'Jess, will you translate?' I said.

She nodded, and then she started to twitch.

24

Octo-Rage

'For a long time, I thought I wanted to be an octopus – content to be solitary, free of friends, or a partner, or offspring. Free of family. But, a few months ago, things started to change. I got involved in the affairs of those who shared the space around me, with Alex and with Jess, and with their concerns. I started to feel warmly towards them. I started to care. And then I met Elle, who propelled me into an entirely new life of companionship. It was challenging, having feelings of attachment but, after great contemplation on the matter, I have to acknowledge that the good outweighs the bad.

'I recently asked Alex and Jess to teach me about family, and at first what I saw made me want to swim away and never come back. But, over time, I have started to think differently. These are the things I know about family. Family is the word for a group of people who are joined by an invisible thread. They might all be similar, or very different. They might disagree, and fight, and say cruel things in anger but, at the end of it all, they will always defend one another and try to keep each other from harm. Families aren't just made up of those you are born to – people from outside can find a way in and be just as important. When someone becomes part of your family, you give them a place in your heart. No matter how much time passes, and no matter what happens, that place is theirs always. They will always be loved. They can never be replaced.'

Bob swam down to Suki, so close that she could kill him in an instant.

'I'm very sorry, but if this man says he could replace you, then you don't have a place in his heart. He is not your family.'

It was probably the most moving speech I've ever heard in my life and I felt tears sting my eyes. There was a stunned silence as Bob's words sank in.

'What a load of nonsense!' Montgomery McMonaghan laughed. 'Now I'm going to especially enjoy flushing you.'

Suki jetted up from the bottom of the tank so that she was level with his head, her black eyes boring into him. And her skin started to change colour. Jess's eyes widened as she realised what my plan was. She picked up a chair, and in an awesome slow-motion sequence, she swung it back and smashed it into the glass wall, full force. It should have been awesome. Unfortunately, the chair bounced back, flew out of Jess's hands and smashed into one of the cabinets instead.

'You two are simply adorable,' McMonaghan laughed. 'But I'm afraid we're going to have to end this here.'

'Wait! I didn't show you my weapon yet,' I said, pulling my hand out of my pocket, with the laser wrapped tightly in my fist. 'The laser might not blast through glass, but if the AAAA handbook is correct – and it is always correct – all I have to do is use this pointed end…' I held it up and walked to the edge of the aquarium wall, '...and bash it hard, right about here.'

I stabbed the laser into the glass as hard as I could, praying to Thor that it would work. And I heard a crack. It looked small at first, just a few centimetres long, but then, with a horrific noise, the crack splintered quickly across the glass. I jumped back as the whole aquarium wall exploded outwards, carrying a lake load of water, coral and fish with it. And at the front of it all, spear-heading the charge was Suki, now bright yellow with neon blue and black rings all over her skin. She flung herself at McMonaghan, landing on his face.

'Help me block the door,' I said, and me, Jess and Dave pushed the desk in front of it.

'Jess, get the fish into the holding tank. Dave, finish up with the files.'

'Do you really think you can stop me?' Montgomery McMonaghan roared, throwing Suki to the ground and flying towards me with his hands outstretched, reaching for my throat.

He grabbed for me, his hands like pincers around my neck and I struggled for breath. But I managed to splutter out a laugh. 'She bit you,' I said.

'I hardly felt it,' he said.

'But you will in a few seconds,' I said, and his hands suddenly dropped.

He looked down at them, horrified. 'I can't move them.'

'As I'm sure you know, her toxin paralyses people for hours before it leaves their body,' I smiled. 'It only works when she's angry, and you made her really, *really* angry.'

The sound of people hammering on the door almost ruined my enjoyment of the moment. We had to get out of there.

'I'm done,' Dave said, hitting a button on the computer, then helping Jess to collect the fish and throw them into the holding tank. It was a bit of a crush in there but at least they'd be safe. Jess had put Bob in his jar and he was watching from one of the bookshelves. As McMonaghan collapsed to the floor, Suki crawled over and sat on his chest, refusing to move.

'That's you done,' I said to McMonaghan. His body was still but he could just about move his face.

'Shame about your mother and grandmother,' he said, doing a weird throaty gargle that I think was a laugh.

'What do you mean?' Jess said. 'Tell us now!'

'Clean up,' he said. 'Already in motion.'

'We'll fix it,' I shouted.

'Too late.' His face was becoming more and more frozen.

We had to make him tell us his plan, and we only had seconds. I searched my mind for something we could use – some leverage.

'Do you know what your dad said about you?' I said. 'He told us he was proud of how smart and successful you are.'

'And that he wishes he'd made more of an effort with you when you were younger,' Jess added.

'I know you care about him, so you might be interested to know that he's joined the Zumba class. Anything you have planned for them will happen to him, too.'

McMonaghan looked stricken. It was the first time I'd really seen him crack. He tried to speak, but the toxin had done its job and he was frozen. All he managed was one word: 'Flash.'

'The flash mob,' Jess gasped. 'He's set something up for the flash mob!'

A sick feeling spread through my body – Mum and Nanny were in real danger. 'We need to get there, now.'

'This way.' Dave grabbed our bags and pushed us through the broken glass to the room beyond the aquarium. 'I looked at the floor plans – there's a way out.'

We ran as fast as we could through the next room, which had two exits. Dave led us to a door in the corner. It took us into a narrow corridor and then to a steep, dark staircase. When we got to the bottom, we found a door marked Fire Exit. Dave pushed the bar, making the fire alarm go off, but we ignored it and ran out into the grounds. The sky had grown dark and there was a rumble of thunder in the air as we crossed the courtyard, sprinted down the gravel drive and made it out onto the street.

'What are we going to do now?' I said, without breaking my stride. 'We don't have time to wait for a bus – it'll take ages.'

'We have to warn them. Phone your mum!' Jess gasped, pulling her own phone out of her pocket and scrolling through her recent calls. 'I'll see if my mum can pick us up.'

'Already calling the police,' Dave said, with his phone to his ear.

Have you ever tried using the phone while

running for your life? Well, let me tell you, it isn't easy at all. My fingers kept slipping on the screen and I nearly dropped it about twenty times before I finally hit Mum's name and heard it ringing.

'Please answer,' I said. 'Please answer, please answer, please answer.'

But she didn't answer.

I tried Nanny next, but she didn't answer either. Neither did Dad.

'They must be at the flash-mob event already,' Jess said. 'They probably can't hear their phones. I can't get my mum either.'

'My mum's at work,' said Dave, 'so I won't be able to get hold of her easily.'

'Who else can we call?' I said, feeling like I might cry. 'There must be someone who can help us.'

We were nearly at the bus stop and there was no sign of a bus coming.

'Argh!' I shouted. 'I. Hate. Buses!'

'The police said they'll look into it.' Dave hung up his phone. 'But I'm pretty sure they think I was pranking them.'

'And no one else from Zumba will hear their phones either.' I stopped running and bent over, putting my hands on my knees, trying not to be sick. 'We need someone close by, who has a car, and is definitely not at the Zumba event.'

'Da'Shon!' Jess said. 'His number is on his website, and he has a car.'

'Your nanny said they let him go home from the police station, as long as he stays away from all the Zumba people,' said Dave. 'He'll get in trouble if he goes to the flash mob event.'

'But there's no one else, and I know he'll want to help us! Call him, Jess,' I jumped up and down. 'Call him!'

Jess punched in the number and put her phone to her ear while Dave and I watched and waited.

'Hello, Da'Shon?' Jess said. 'It's Jess and Alex from Zumba class. I'm sorry to bother you, but we really need your help – everyone from Zumba is in danger.'

I couldn't hear what Da'Shon said, but it wasn't much because with no arguments or explanations, within thirty seconds, Jess had told him where we were and, ten minutes later, we saw his car speeding towards us. His brakes squealed as he pulled up beside us.

'You guys OK?' he said. 'Jump in.'

We practically threw ourselves into the car and Da'Shon waited only for us to put our seatbelts on before taking off down the road towards Cherry Tree Lane.

'Where are we headed?' he said.

'We need to get to the flash-mob event in the park.'

'We'll be there in ten,' he said. 'Don't worry.'

We drove in silence for a moment, lost in our own thoughts.

'You guys want to fill me in on what's going on?' Da'Shon said. 'So I can help?'

'It's a long story,' I said. 'But, basically, we found out that something weird was happening with the ladies in the Zumba class, and that's why we joined.'

'And there was me thinking it was because of my irresistible charm and charisma.' I saw Da'Shon smile in the mirror.

'At first we thought it might be you doing something to them,' I said. 'And we're really sorry about that.'

'I can see how you might suspect me,' he said.

'But we realised it wasn't you ages ago,' Jess said.

'And we wanted to find out who was really

behind it so that we could help the class and get you out of trouble,' I added.

'Thanks for believing in me.' Da'Shon paused, took a breath, then carried on. 'Especially after I kept things hidden from you.'

'You had your reasons,' Dave said. 'It doesn't matter now.'

'You know everyone from Zumba has been going crazy trying to clear your name. Mum and Nanny have started a campaign and everything.'

'Ah, man, that means a lot.' He laughed, and it was like having the old Da'Shon back. 'They're the greatest crew anyone could ever ask for.'

'And now they're in proper danger,' I said. 'The super-villain behind all of it – messing with the Zumbies...'

'That's what we call the Zumba ladies,' Jess interrupted.

'...And framing you – has some kind of plan in action to destroy all the evidence against him.'

'And the Zumbies,' Jess said. 'They're...'

'...Evidence too,' Da'Shon said.

'We know you're not allowed near the flash-mob event,' said Dave. 'But if you could just drop us off by the park?'

‘Nah. I appreciate your concern, but this is too serious. Those people are my family. If they’re in danger then I’m coming to help. Even if it means going back to jail.’

If he hadn’t been driving at dangerously high speed, I legit would have kissed him.

A drop of rain spattered on the windscreen, and Da’Shon screeched the car to a stop. We were at Rocket Park.

25

Jess Finally Lets It Go

We swung the car doors open and jumped out, leaving our bags and Bob on the back seat. Da'Shon got out too, and we faced the Rocket Park together. He looked so different out of his Zumba gear. He was wearing dark jeans and a black tracksuit jacket, zipped all the way to the top, with his hood up and pulled tight around his face. The park gate was open and decorated with balloons which were being buffeted around by the wind. I could hear music blasting and, though the sky was getting darker by the second, there was a glow coming from the park.

'Where the hell did those come from?' Jess said, pointing to some grey metal poles looming above the trees, each one topped with a huge light and speaker. Giant silver balloons were rising up around them and disappearing into the stormy clouds.

'I've never seen balloons like that before,' I said.

'Looks like *War of the Worlds*,' Da'Shon said. 'This is crazy.

'I think they're weather balloons.' Dave squinted up at the sky.

As we watched, one of the balloons burst, exploding in a bright pink mist, like a firework.

'I have a really bad feeling about this,' I yelled, as we ran down the path and into the park. There we stopped. There were people everywhere, most of them of the older variety and wearing leggings.

'Looks like word of the flash mob really got out,' I said. 'It's packed. How are we going to find Mum and Nanny?'

'I think the bandstand is at the centre of it all,' Dave said. 'Let's try to get there – if we can get up, we'll have a better view.' He started gently tapping people on the shoulder and saying 'excuse me, please,' really politely. Because it was noisy, and lots of them were quite old and didn't have the best ears, most of them had to ask him to repeat himself.

'This is taking way too long,' Jess huffed. 'Elbows, everyone. But only at twenty-five per cent strength. We don't want to damage any of them.'

We dived into the crowd, ignoring lots of tutting and shaking of heads. I twisted my head in every direction, but I couldn't see Mum, Nanny, or anyone else from our class.

'Don't forget to look out for anything suspicious,' I shouted. 'McMonaghan has something planned – something to destroy any evidence of what he did to the Zumbies.'

'We have no idea what, though!' Jess yelled. 'It could be right in front of our eyes and we wouldn't even know it.'

A big drop of rain sploshed on my face, and I shouted in frustration. We were at the back of the bandstand now, but the crowd was so thick here, it would take ages to push around to the other side. And we were missing something.

We stopped against the back wall of the bandstand, and got squished against it by the throng of people, who were all laughing, singing and having shouted conversations. None of them aware of the danger they were in.

'We're running out of time,' I yelled.

'You can't know that, Alex – we don't know when whatever is going to be happening is supposed to happen,' Jess shouted back.

'Can't you feel it, though?' I said. 'The looming threat. The sense of doom.'

'This is not the time to be dramatic,' Jess said.

'It's just the weather,' Dave said. 'There's a storm coming.'

I looked up as I felt more droplets splash onto my hat and coat. I watched another shiny balloon burst among the clouds in a puff of neon pink, making all the Zumbies cheer. And I understood.

'The floodlight towers,' I said. 'Look at them! Look at how they're set out!'

Jess, Dave and Da'Shon all looked up and saw what I saw. The light towers were the tallest things in the park – and probably the tallest things for miles around. And they were set out in a circle, with a giant Christmas tree at the back, enclosing everyone who was there for the Zumba flash mob. The Christmas tree was topped with an over-sized metallic star, which had an extra-long point reaching upwards like a spire of doom.

'They're lightning rods,' Dave gasped.

'And the balloons must have been made by the geo-engineers,' Jess said. 'They're helping to build the storm!'

'The psychotic son of a biscuit is going to electrocute the Zumbies,' I said.

'And everyone else with them,' Da'Shon added.

Another rumble of thunder shook the sky.

'We need to get everyone out of here now,' Da'Shon said. 'Let's get on this bandstand. Can you guys climb?'

It was a few metres up but Da'Shon gave me and Jess a boost. We used the patterns on the sides of the bandstand as hand and foot holds and gripped as hard as we could with our freezing fingertips. Dave was surprisingly athletic and made it look easy. He pulled himself over the barrier that ran around the edge, then reached down to give us a hand. I made a note to myself to practise climbing fences more so that I wouldn't have to embarrass myself again. Eventually I dragged myself over and landed in the centre of the bandstand looking out over the flash mob. In front of us was a sound system and a Zumba teacher in neon-pink sportswear standing with her back to us, doing some stretches.

'Hey!' I shouted. 'We have an emergency situation and need your help.'

She turned around with an annoyed look on her face. It was Angel.

'Participants need to be down there,' she pointed. 'The flash mob will start in fifteen minutes.'

'We need to get everyone out of here,' I said. 'Right now.'

'No chance.' She stood there with her hands on her hips. 'I've been instructed to ensure this event takes place no matter what.'

'You work for McMonaghan,' Jess said. 'Don't you?'

'Get off the bandstand,' Angel hissed.

'But he's setting you up – if you stay here, you'll die.' I said. 'We need to tell everyone – give us the microphone.'

'I've been given this microphone because I'm leading the flash mob. Get out of my way.' She shoved me back.

I looked at Jess. This wasn't working – there was no way Angel would give up the microphone without a fight, and without it we had no hope of getting everyone's attention.

'These ladies are my students.' Da'Shon stepped towards her, pulling his hood down and unzipping his tracksuit top. 'And if anyone's going to lead them in the flash mob, it's me.' He whipped off his trousers and jacket to reveal his full Zumba kit – tight vest and short shorts, both black but with neon orange stripes down the side.

'You're not allowed to be here,' Angel said. 'I'll call the police!'

'You do that,' Da'Shon said. 'And we'll let the ladies decide who they want to run this flash mob.'

At that moment, a couple of people looked towards the bandstand and saw him. I saw them gasp and smile, then nudge the people next to them, and it rippled through the crowd until, after just a few minutes, everyone was looking our way. Then someone – and even though I couldn't see her, I'm pretty certain it was Nanny – started a chant. 'Da'Shon, Da'Shon, Da'Shon…' and one by one, they took off their jackets and hoodies to reveal their 'Free Da'Shon' T-shirts.

Angel looked out across the sea of Da'Shons, the chanting so loud that it drowned out the thunder. She was beaten and she knew it. She took off the headset, threw it on the floor and stomped on it with the ferocity of Jess when she sees a celebrity wearing a fur coat, before pushing her way off the bandstand. Da'Shon stood facing the crowd – every pair of eyes shining with happiness at seeing him there; every voice singing his name – and his eyes filled with tears. It was a moment I'll never forget for as long as I live.

But we were running out of time. The rain was falling heavily now. The storm was almost upon us.

'The headset's broken,' Jess shouted, picking it up off the floor. 'The mic doesn't work. How are we going to tell them they're in danger?'

'Listen, everyone!' I shouted. 'We need you to move! Get out of the park now!'

But nobody was listening. Lightning crackled in the sky, somewhere in the distance, and I knew what we had to do.

'Can we skip to the flash-mob track?' I asked Dave, pointing to the music system.

'Let me check,' he said, running across to it and crouching down at the controls.

'We're not actually doing the flash mob, are we?' Jess looked horrified.

'They're Zumbies, Jess,' I said. 'Dancing is written into their memories. We can use that.'

Dave nodded at us.

'Da'Shon,' I said. 'You need to dance. But not on the spot like normal Zumba – lead the herd out of the circle to safety.'

'I got this,' he said. 'Let's go.'

Jess signalled to Dave and the flash-mob track started to play, the bass making the bandstand beneath us shake as the music blared across the park. As I'd hoped, the Zumbies instantly began to move, following the choreography with pinpoint precision. They were perfectly in sync, like they'd been CGI'd – every shoulder roll, foot flick and switch-kick a thing of awesomeness.

'We've got to get them on *Britain's Got Talent*,' I said. 'They'll kill it.'

Da'Shon did the routine with them, the rain glistening on his skin, slowly making his way down the steps of the bandstand and into the crowd. The Zumbies parted to give him space, never missing a step, and then followed as he led them across the grass and away from the lightning rods.

'Not the quickest escape I've ever seen,' I said.

'But definitely the most beautiful.' Jess gazed at the dancing herd as they transitioned into the first chorus.

'He's like the Pied Piper of Zumbies,' I said, watching in awe as they gyrated and booty shook across the park.

Lightning split the sky again, much closer this time, and some of the Zumbies stopped dancing to look at it.

'No,' I shouted. 'They were so close!'

'It's the electricity,' Jess said. 'They're drawn to it, and Da'Shon is so far away they can't see him anymore.'

'I need to find Mum and Nanny before it's too late. You'll have to get down there, Jessticles,' I said. 'Draw their attention with the dance. Keep leading them out past the Christmas tree.'

'What?' she gasped. 'No!'

'You have to, Jess.'

'But I honestly can't, Alex. There must be another way.'

She looked terrified. The girl who stood up to bullies without a moment's hesitation. The girl who saved us from my ex-friend Jason, Miss

Smilie and Taran. The girl who just desecrated the shoe of the most intelligent, evil, powerful man in the world. I'd seen her run straight towards danger a hundred times, without seeming even the tiniest bit scared. And she was afraid to dance. I breathed in the smell of wet grass and sweat, closed my eyes and took her hand, wondering how I could convince her. 'It could be their only chance, Jess – if you don't dance them away, they're going to get hurt. They might even die. You're the bravest person I know and I need you to do this. Remember what Da'Shon said: let yourself go.'

She swallowed. Nodded. Took off her coat and ran down the steps until she was standing in front of the main group of Zumbies. And then, with the wind whipping around her, she danced. She threw out every bit of her moody, serious, ferocious self and became something I'd never seen before – she was totally free.

'Wow, Jess unleashed,' I said, as she shimmied into the Bollywood hands section. Don't get me wrong, she was absolutely rubbish – she moved like a supermarket trolley with a dodgy wheel, and her Bollywood hands looked more like a glitching robot trying to give itself a high five. But it didn't matter.

The Zumbies started to move with her, metre by metre, through the circle of death towards safety. But as I watched, their hair began to float upwards until it was standing on end, like what happens when you get static from a balloon. The lightning was coming.

'Dave, get out!' I shouted. 'Now!'

'What about you?' he called back.

'I'm coming,' I shouted. 'Right behind you!'

Most of the Zumbies were through, now, getting further away from the danger. But then I saw something that made my heart sink in my chest. It was Mum and Nanny, right at the back of the crowd, waving. They'd waited behind for me.

'Run!' I shouted, trying to compete with the storm. They couldn't hear me. I jumped off the bandstand, missing half the steps, landing on the concrete below and grazing my knee. Thunder boomed directly over my head and I knew this was it. They weren't going to make it. They seemed to realise the danger just at that last second, because they started to run towards me. I could see their mouths opening as they screamed at me, but I couldn't make out what they were saying.

We were almost at the edge of the circle. But there was a crackling in the air, and Mum's and Nanny's hair was standing right up, like they were hanging upside down. I was aware of the crash of thunder and rain lashing into my face. Nanny was just outside the circle now, but not Mum – she was still inside, reaching towards me. Lightning split the sky and I leapt, putting every bit of energy, anger and frustration into that jump. I crashed into Mum, launching us both out of the circle, just as the lightning hit.

There was a boom – an explosion louder even than the deafening thunder. Out of the corner of my eye I saw something go up in flames. And as I pushed Mum to safety, I became aware of a shadow falling over me.

I turned around to see prickly pine needles, tinsel and baubles. No lights now because everything had gone out. The Christmas tree was falling towards me and I couldn't get out of the way. All I could think was: 'So this is it – this is how I die.' Then everything went dark.

26

Aftermath

So that was the end of my story. I made the ultimate sacrifice, giving my life for my mum's and dying a hero under the weight of a giant Christmas tree. Nah, not really. I had a concussion and I was badly scratched, but I was alright by the next day. Mum was fussing over me, and Nanny was banging on about Yorkshire puddings and pigs in blankets, so it was basically back to normal in our house.

Jess had bad aches from her danceathon, but not so bad that she couldn't hit me really hard every time I did an impression of her at the Zumba flash mob. She'd called the RSPCA about Suki and the fish in McMonaghan's aquarium, reporting that they were being held in unsuitable conditions. Dave sent all the evidence he'd taken from Montgomery McMonaghan to the police, anonymously, of course, and he'd spent the rest of his time worrying about what to get Jess for Christmas, which was a far more scary worry than facing down a super-villain. Dexter kept an eye on McMonaghan's HQ, and told us that after receiving the evidence we collected, the police hadn't taken long to come knocking on his door. He was recovering from the octopus poisoning but we were confident they had enough proof to game-end him for good. The RSPCA also turned up to rescue Suki, who had calmed down enough to return to her un-poisonous colour, and was happy to be re-homed in an aquarium in London.

Bob was back in the tank with Elle, and they were busy planning their future together. And Mr Prickles was, well, Mr Prickles – still the bravest, sweetest, most wonderful little dude in my life.

Everything was pretty great – it felt like the storm had passed.

A week later it was Christmas Day – officially my favourite day of the year. This year we were doing things differently. Instead of getting up and opening presents, we all went over to the cricket club and got to work.

At 1pm, our guests started to arrive.

'Spending Mr McMonaghan's charitable donation on this dinner for everyone was a brilliant idea,' Jess said as we looked around us at the packed room, full of people eating, laughing and celebrating. As well as my family, Jess's mum was there, chatting to Da'Shon while Eileen pulled a cracker with him. Alan sat with Mrs Spires, who was actually laughing for once. Everyone from Zumba was there, and everyone else from Cherry Tree Lane who had wanted to come – we'd sent the invitation out to the whole street. It turns out that lots of people feel lonely at Christmas, and this was our way of showing them that they weren't alone.

'I'm a bit worried about Nanny and Mr McMonaghan,' I said. 'Nanny's acting really strange. Do you think he's actually evil after all and has done something weird to her?'

'You really don't know anything, do you?' Jess snorted. 'She's flirting with him.'

'What?!' I looked at them in horror. Nanny was giggling and touching his arm. 'Is Mr McMonaghan going to be my new grandad?'

'I reckon so,' Jess said. 'And it's all thanks to you.'

'What have I done?' I pulled my hat off and held it over my eyes. 'Make it stop, Jessticles!'

'Alex,' Jess nudged me. 'She's here! She's come!'

I put my hat back on and looked towards the door. Miss Fortress had just walked in. We ran over as fake-casually as possible. But when we were standing in front of her, watching her eyes shine as she gazed around the room, for once I didn't know what to say.

'Thank you for inviting me – this looks wonderful,' Miss Fortress said.

'Nobody should be on their own at Christmas, Miss,' said Jess.

'I know it's not the same as being able to go home,' I said, 'but you should know that you will always have family in Cherry Tree Lane.'

'We saved you a seat over here.' I beckoned her over to the end of one of the tables. 'And we have a present for you. It's on your seat.'

'A present?' She blinked.

'Just go see,' Jess said. And we followed her to

her seat, where a tatty-looking cat, who in spite of her appearance still managed to have the air of a diva, was sitting, licking her paws.

Miss Fortress stopped. Gasped. 'It can't be.' She stepped forward. 'Glory?'

The cat, who we now knew was called Glory, looked up at Miss Fortress. There was a moment of stillness, like when you go to the cinema and you've sat through all the ads and trailers and then the curtains open wider and the title screen comes up. An awesome moment of anticipation – knowing something amazing is coming. And then Glory flew with the grace of a Jedi into Miss Fortress's open arms and Miss Fortress kissed her a million times, in between sobs.

'How did you find her?' Miss Fortress said.

'I'm glad you asked, Miss,' I said. 'There were a few things really – we knew you used to have someone in your life that you missed – someone that Montgomery McMonaghan took from you somehow. We also knew that he deliberately led us to the photo in this cricket club, which meant he had leverage over someone here. After he was arrested, we came here and spoke to Glory. She told us everything.

'Thank you both, so, so much,' Miss Fortress said. And she looked like a different person from the uptight professor we'd been working with for so long.

Me and Jess sat at the same corner table we'd had for Mrs Spires' funeral, with plates piled high with food in front of us.

'Time for a debrief,' I said. Jess groaned. 'I feel like we've both learnt a lot during this mission.'

'So, what have you learnt, Alex? That you should be nicer to your mum?'

'Yes – that,' I said. 'But lots of other things, too. I've learnt not to judge people without getting to know them first. The Zumba class, Da'Shon, Mr McMonaghan – they were all totally different from what I'd expected.'

'Yeah, you underestimate everybody, generally,' Jess said.

'I've learnt that my lie detector can be used, not just to find out who's guilty, but also to find out who's innocent – and that's possibly even more important.'

'Also true.'

'And, finally, I have learnt that you are the most horrible dancer on the planet.'

I braced myself for the inevitable whack, but it didn't come.

'Harsh, but fair,' Jess said.

It seemed almost impossible for my human mind to grasp, but maybe Jess had learnt something too.

She lifted her glass of lemonade and smiled at me. 'Best Christmas ever?'

I clinked my glass against hers and smiled back. 'Best Christmas ever.'

Also by Jennifer Killick

Alex Sparrow and the Really Big Stink
Alex Sparrow and the Furry Fury

Mo, Lottie and the Junkers

Coming spring 2020
Crater Lake

Coming Soon

CRATER LAKE

Welcome to **Crater Lake**: the Year Six school trip from hell!

Maybe it's the mysterious bloodstained man who tries to stop their coach, or the way no one turns up to meet them at the brand-new activity centre when Lance and his class arrive, but something is definitely not right at Crater Lake.

Then, on the first night, things get stranger…

Instructions for Crater Lake

Do: Take plenty of rations; the food's pretty awful.

Do: Work out quickly who your friends and enemies are.

Don't: Panic about being in a creepy new activity centre built in an old volcanic crater miles from anywhere, and above all

DON'T: Ever. Fall. Asleep!

CRATER LAKE

Excerpt from Chapter 1

...'Year six – I want everyone to quiet down and face the front.' Miss Hoche, the assistant head, stands up at the front of the coach, trying not to fall as it bumps up the country road. I always think saying her name sounds like you're trying to cough up something nasty, which works because it's how she makes me feel.

'I'm now going to provide you with some information,' she says, pronouncing the long words especially slowly and clearly for those of us who are too dumb to understand people speaking at normal speed – aka me, or so she thinks.

'This information is of the greatest importance for ensuring you have a safe and productive trip. Some of you...' (she looks at me) '... should be paying particular attention to the information about the rules.'

If she says 'information' one more time…

'There will be stickers presented to the children who demonstrate exemplary behaviour,' she beams at Trent, Adrianne and Chets. 'And punishments for those who let the rest of the class down by being disruptive.' I'll give you one guess who she looks at when she says that.

She opens a leaflet and starts to read. 'Crater Lake is a new and innovative activity centre, designed with the needs and safety of your children in mind to provide an unforgettable learning experience.' She looks up. 'We're actually the first school to be trying out this centre, so we're extremely fortunate.'

'My mum is a parent governor,' Trent says, loud enough so I will hear, 'and she told me we're stuck going to Crater Lake because some people's scummy parents refused to pay for the good activity centres.' More laughing from the jerks at the back.

'The centre was built deep in rural Sussex, in a crater thought to have been formed when a meteor hit the earth's surface hundreds of years ago,' Hoche continues.

'A meteor from space, Miss?' someone asks.

'Yes, of course. Where else would a meteor come from?'

'A meaty rowing boat,' Big Mak whispers from the seat in front of me and we crack up.

Miss Hoche glares at us.

'The deepest part of the crater is home to Crater Lake itself, as the River Whist, which used to run past the site, took a detour many years ago and now feeds into the crater. The lake is the ideal arena for many of our daring water activities, such as swimming, canoeing and our epic game, "The Last Man Standing".'

'So sexist,' Adrianne sighs. Adrianne is Head Girl, super smart and looks kind of like an angry sparrow. You wouldn't mess with her. If anyone in our class is going to win a game called Last Man Standing, I'd bet everything I own that it would be Adrianne.

'Other outdoor activities include the climbing wall, obstacle course and the Leap Of Faith.'

'I don't like the sound of that,' Chets says.

'Chets,' I say, putting my hand on his arm for added reassurance, 'they're not going to let us do anything even slightly dangerous.'

'That's true,' Katja nods. 'There are laws.'

'I heard you have to jump over a ravine filled with starving crocodiles,' Big Mak says. Chets looks horrified.

'The dormitories, chill-out zone...' (the whole class rolls their eyes) '...dining hall and bathrooms are located in the main building, which is built on a rise in the crater.' At this point I start to slip into a coma. Miss Hoche always says at least a hundred more things than are necessary.

'Do I have your attention, Lance Sparshott?' She's suddenly standing right in front of my seat.

'Yes, Miss.'

She leans in way too close to my face. I'm in the window seat, so Chets has to squash himself into the back of his seat to avoid any uncomfortable physical contact. Her breath smells like coffee and muddy dog. 'You're lucky to be on this trip. If there was any way I could prove what we both know you did at the beginning of the year, you would have been excluded. If you take even the smallest step out of line, you'll be done, and there will be a black mark on your school record before you've even started at Latham High.'

She withdraws from mine and Chets' seating area, like a swamp monster oozing back into its pit, and starts walking towards the front of the coach again. Chets is frozen, burrowed so far into the padding of the seat that if his skin was some weird purple and blue triangular print, he'd be totally camouflaged.

'Bit too close for you?' I say.

'No words,' he mutters, without blinking.

Katja giggles, and Big Mak coughs to cover a snort of laughter.

'Something funny?' Miss Hoche spins round.

We all look at the floor.

'Stickers for everyone for excellent listening,' Miss Hoche says. 'Except Lance, Maksym and Katja.'

Yeah, no listening stickers for us – that punishment really burns.

'The rules of Crater Lake are as follows.' She nearly falls as she wobbles back to her seat where she left the leaflet. Katja and Big Mak are desperately trying not to laugh. Chets is motionless. Probably still in shock.

'Six children – either boys or girls, not both – to a room...'

(Please don't say what I know you're going to say, Hoche).

'Except for Lance, who has to have his own room due to personal issues.'

Whispers and sniggers all around. I hate her.

'Nobody is to enter a dormitory other than their

own. You must remain in your rooms throughout the night. Mr Tomkins, Miss Rani and myself will be watching at all times.' She pauses to stare around at all of us, just to remind us how good she is at watching.

'Never wander the site alone,' she continues. 'You must always be accompanied by a member of staff.'

Sucking the fun right out of everything as usual.

'You must follow any and all instructions given to you by a member of staff. This is for your own safety.'

Chets nods enthusiastically.

'And of course – have fun! Your experience at Crater Lake is going to be one you'll remember for the rest of your lives.'

She smiles – I think she's waiting for us to clap or something.

There's an awkward moment of silence and then stuff gets crazy…

Acknowledgements

To Penny, Meg, Janet, Rebecca and Simone at Firefly Press: I feel extraordinarily fortunate to be working with the most passionate and supportive publishing team I could wish for. Thank you for everything. To my super-agent, Kirsty: I am so grateful for your wisdom and guidance. Thank you to Heath McKenzie and Alex Dimond for another awesome cover.

To incredible author friends: Lorraine, Vashti, Eloise, Ness and BB: thank you for your wonderful support and encouragement – you are all such stars. To Imogen at Golden Egg: thank you, as always, for helping me to find my way with my writing and for setting me on this path. To brilliant bookish people, Jo Clarke and Jo Cummins, and amazing Waterstones booksellers, Jane, Angelica, Tom, Lauren, Lance, Heather and Kate at Uxbridge, Karen at Cirencester, and Fiona at Durham: thank you for your amazing support. To the Reading

Agency who have embraced my books from the start, and the librarians who get them into the hands of readers: your support has meant the world – thank you.

Working with schools is one of the best parts of my job, and I'm extremely grateful to every school, teacher and child who has welcomed me. I have met so many inspirational teachers who have put my books into their classes and libraries, but I would like to especially thank Bruce McInnes, Ashley Booth, Ian Hunt, Karl Duke, Julie Killick, Neil Black, Tami Wylie, Julie Bennett, Matthew Girvan, Jane Clapp, Maaria Khan, Sophie Topliss, Richard Long, Scott Evans and everyone at Colham Manor. Huge thanks to the children of Little Plumstead who named Snuffles the dog, and massive thank you squeezes to every one of the wonderful readers who provided such lovely quotes for the cover of this book.

To Mum, Dad, Julie and Alfie who I couldn't manage without, and to my husband Dean, who keeps me steady as I try to negotiate the rollercoaster: thank you. Lots of love and thanks go to my children, Stanley, Teddy, Mia, Helena and Luis, who refuse to read my books themselves but want to fight anyone who says anything mean about them. Thank you to my friends, Nic, Laura, Emma, Sarah and Jay, for always being there. And finally, thank you, thank you, thank you, to everyone who has taken the time to read one of my books. I hope you enjoyed reading this story as much as I enjoyed writing it.